HANGING O[N]

Sarah Baird-Smith

Constable · London

First published in Great Britain 1995
by Constable and Company
3, The Lanchesters, 162 Fulham Palace Road
London W6 9ER
Copyright © 1995 The Estate of Sarah Baird-Smith
ISBN 0 09 474290 1
Set in Linotron Baskerville 11pt by
CentraCet Ltd, Cambridge
Printed in Great Britain by
St Edmundsbury Press Ltd
Bury St Edmunds, Suffolk

A CIP catalogue record for this book
is available from the British Library

FOR MAX AND LEONORA

CHAPTER 1

Five thirty on a blustery September afternoon. Polly Lonsdale walked out of the wind into the wide hall and dropped her keys onto the side-table under the big mirror, her mink onto a chair. It slid to the floor, where she left it. Edward, her tidy husband, would have been horrified, but she felt a day so well organised should have a little anarchy thrown into it, and anyway, dear patient Sandra would put it away.

She'd bought all the uniform for yet another school for Muffy, remembered to take her pearls and her ex-mother-in-law's amber necklace for restringing in the Burlington Arcade, met up successfully with Ruth, her best friend, for lunch at Fortnum's and the exhibition of Norwegian paintings at the Royal Academy. She'd even found a taxi with a non-communicative driver to take her back from Harrods to Connaught Square. Now there was the weekend at Cottenham to look forward to. Jessica would come home tonight, back from her course in Canterbury, and they would all drive up tomorrow. Robert, Jess's fiancé, would join them on Saturday.

'How were the Scandiwegians? Did anyone spit at you in that coat? Did you get all my stuff, Mum?' Sixteen-year-old Muffy edged down the stairs.

'No, they didn't, though some women did shout. And yes, lovey, I did. It cost a fortune and I hope to God it fits. Try it on. Hideous colours again, I'm afraid, but there we are. Now, no more running away.'

'Mum, I never run away – well, I didn't last time.'

'No, you didn't need to, darling, the way you carried on. No wonder poor Mother Superior chucked you out, writing that letter about convent education. Why the *Independent* had to print it, I don't know. For Christ's sake, Muffs, do try to stay around this time, or Edward will have a fit.'

'And Mother Madeleine would have a fit to hear your language, Ma.' Muffy the virtuous departed upstairs with the bulging green-and-gold bags, and Polly looked affectionately after her. If Muffy weren't so clever, her capacity for exhausting the patience of boarding-school headmistresses might be quite worrying. Sending her to a convent had been a new departure; remembering her own convent days, Polly had had high hopes . . . Ah well. With a sigh she picked up the mail from the hall table and went into the drawing-room.

Apart from the ambassadorial monstrosity on the corner, theirs was the best house in the square; this delighted Polly. She was a great snob for quality – well, she didn't like to be outdone. She had, after all, made it, and she wanted their large circle of friends and the rest of the world to know.

The house was double-fronted, with a long drawing-room to the right of the door, dining-room and kitchen on the left. Upstairs was the master bedroom, appropriately large. Bed, bath and dressing-room were in proportion. Muffy had clung ferociously to her room opposite, and Edward had his study beyond. There was a pretty spare room on the floor above – next to the still intact nursery – and the room Jessica, Polly's nineteen-year-old, had moved into when she and Muffy grew too old to share. Sandra, their housekeeper, had a flat in the basement.

Nor was this the only establishment over which Polly presided. As well as a desirable London house full of (rather overfull of) important furniture, rugs and pictures, there was also its equivalent in the country: a rosy-bricked, mullion-windowed Jacobean manor house at Cottenham in Suffolk which Edward had inherited from his mother, and to which they all regularly repaired at weekends. And furthermore there was a château in central France: rather small, but a château all the same, and the scene of many happy family holidays.

Lucky Polly, then, the mistress of so much. And then there was trusty Sandra, the envy of her friends, always at hand, so that she had the liberty, as well as the money, to shop, lunch with friends and admirers, visit the hairdresser. True, there had been the problems with Jessica – the physiotherapy course didn't seem to be a great success, and she was still doubtful about Robert, but Jess was so much better now. And Muffy was a dear, even if she was a bit of a handful. Two more or less satisfactory daughters, and a rich and devoted husband whom she loved. Lucky Polly indeed.

Luckier by far than Ruth, who would be on her way back now to her cottage near Ipswich. Not only did Ruth have the anxiety of a demanding job – she was Features Editor of *House in Style*, one of the proliferating magazines that focused on the homes of the enviably rich – but she had the persistent worry of her sweet but ineffectual husband Harry, who made up for the lack of business his building and design company generated by making endlessly expensive alterations to their cottage. And then there was her beloved but worrying son, Dave, the child of an earlier marriage. Things seemed to be all right there now, though. After school and a spell at some college, both disastrous, he had simply drifted for a few years, but recently, with a mixture of sorrow and relief, Ruth had seen him off to the States, where he apparently worked for a bank. Exactly what he did nobody seemed to know, though on his last visit home it was clear that it paid well: cashmere sweaters and designer sunglasses. He was a changed man from the scruffy youth who used to turn up at Cottenham and whirl Muffy away on his motor bike.

Polly had known Ruth since Jessica was a baby; recalling her familiar plump face over the Fortnum's table now, she thought she had looked even more strained than usual today – but she had had good news to report. Harry had got a job.

'It's over at The Buttocks.' The Gunnocks, an imposing and beautiful Thomas Wyatt mansion not far from Cottenham, had been rechristened years ago by Muffy. 'It's been sold again – the new owner's come over from the States apparently, made a fortune in electronics at the right time; I haven't met him, but he's got a fantastic collection of pictures. You must come and see it, I'll be in there for the mag. Of course, when Harry's finished.' She'd smiled at Polly. 'But how are you? You're quiet today. Must be the paintings – all those silent Nordic wastes.' She looked anxious again. 'It's not the girls, is it?'

Polly had reflected for a moment before answering. She'd always told Ruth everything – well, nearly everything. 'I always worry about Jess, as you know. But actually it's Edward.'

'It can't be his business – I thought that was booming.' Ruth put on her soulful look. 'Polly – it's not a girl, is it?'

'Of course not, Edward's not like that.' Polly's mild irritation evaporated as she tried to find just the right tone of voice in which to say: 'No, he seems to have got religion.'

'Oh?' Ruth, from a liberal Jewish family, had been genuinely interested. 'Which kind? Isn't that all right? I thought his father was a priest or something?'

'Not a priest, priests don't marry. Anyway, it was his grandfather. But this is different; he goes off to prayer meetings, that sort of thing. I found him on his knees by the bed the other night, like Christopher Robin.' Polly giggled. 'And these odd people keep coming round. All very tidy and well-spoken, terrific smiles and sensible hair. Edward disappears into the study with them; I've no idea what goes on . . .'

Polly switched off the memory of her rather uncomfortable conversation with Ruth and sank onto the long sofa in her pretty drawing-room. She idly picked up the tapestry she was working on – a dancing dolphin in a foamy sea – and looked about her with some satisfaction. In here she'd managed to keep the furniture to a minimum, sneaking the more alarming pieces Edward had inherited off to other rooms, or to the attics at Cottenham. She'd thought he wouldn't notice, but he had. But now the rose-and-blue upholstery, the upright chairs with their seats and backs painstakingly embroidered by Edward's grandmother while her husband, the minister, composed his sermons, the remaining pair of rather over-ornate side-tables, all nicely set off her own eclectic collection of Bristol glass and looked delightful in the patchy sunshine which filtered through the heavily draped curtains as the clouds blew about in the wind outside.

She looked through the mail: for her, the usual round of invitations to contribute to this, that and the other, a gallery opening, a party in Highgate – amusing couple, lovely house, but what a trek to get there, she knew Edward would hate it – a couple of thank-yous for a dinner the previous week, a letter from her mother. That could wait – it would be a list of complaints, probably coupled with a none too veiled request for money. After what she herself had been spending recently, she hardly liked to ask Edward for more. He used to give her anything she asked for without question, but he'd actually looked at her recent credit card bill – 'Did you honestly need four new pairs of shoes at once?' – and asked whether the dining-room really needed redecorating after only eighteen months.

'But I always buy all my shoes at the beginning of the season,' she'd lied, smiling up at him with wide eyes – it was quite certain she'd buy at least another four pairs as well – 'and I was fed up with the dining-room, we never should have chosen that dismal green.' For a moment she'd wondered whether his company wasn't doing as well as usual, but she knew that even in the recession, profits were soaring.

Before religion claimed him, Edward's grandfather had been a carpenter, and had started out making pencils; he was soon employing a couple of men to help him, and in the early years of the century took out his savings, borrowed from his local bank and set up a small factory. His foreman had perfected a unique blend of the graphite and clay of which the pencil leads were made; Lonsdale himself travelled extensively to market his wares, and during a trip to Russia obtained the rights to a huge deposit of graphite which ensured the future of the company. His son, Edward's father, had expanded the business; he'd been particularly successful in the growing educational market, becoming sole supplier to the county councils who controlled the centralised orders for equipment.

Edward's father, a small man, had been something of a tyrant in his home. He'd died soon after Edward met Polly; she'd never liked him, sensing his bullying streak, aware of his pretensions. But he'd taken quite a fancy to her and had left her, on his death, a collection of gold snuffboxes, the legacy of the bride he'd brought back from Leningrad, dead since Edward's teens. They were far too valuable (and too ugly) to be on show; with a few photographs and Edward's fluent Russian, they were all that was left of poor Katerina and of old Lonsdale's one romantic moment.

Edward had stood in awe of his father – one of the reasons why he refused to part with any of the solemn Lonsdale furniture. The traditional business continued well, but Edward had also felt that the way lay out of pencils and into the rapidly developing world of computers. After an initial period of indecision he began to make specialised quality electronic drawing instruments and screens for architects, engineers, designers. The success of the move had been confirmed with a recent large order from Japan.

There had been attempts to buy Edward out, which he'd resisted; Polly was sorry, for this would have made him an outright multi-millionaire. As things were, he was, on paper, a rich man, and Polly lacked for nothing except pens and pencils; as is often the way with these things, the samples that probably found their way into the pockets of all the workers never reached the chairman's house.

Polly turned from her own uninteresting mail to Edward's: a bank statement, a letter in a trailing hand which she identified as that of one of his godsons, a few bills, a large, sturdy envelope announcing that it contained the annual report of a company in which he had an interest. She was something of a connoisseur of these documents, and was almost tempted to open it for a laugh at the unfailing portrait photo of a sun-tanned chairman, the reassuring confidence of the board of directors, the smiles on the shop-floor faces pictured in the sparkling interiors of the company's factories. Edward couldn't see why she found these funny – but then it was his money that was involved, and his own company put out a very similar annual handout. She wouldn't open it, though; she had never opened his letters – not yet.

Last, there was a bulky, shiny magazine with a proper spine,

The Christian Businessman, snugly sealed in transparent plastic. The back featured an advertisement for a lap-top computer – free with it, 'The Bible on Disc'. On the front, a man with rather close-set blue eyes showed unnaturally perfect teeth in a smile; the heading 'Jim Drogue tells YOU to go with GROWTH' was reversed out across his dark suit. Polly read on down the contents list: 'Power tactics – evangelise YOUR workplace', 'Christ, credit and crisis – how to control an errant cashflow', 'This Gospel business – harness God's word . . .' The rest of it was obscured by the address label.

Polly sighed – perhaps all this new interest in God was just a passing phase of Edward's, like the time he'd tried to learn Italian. But he wasn't prone to sudden enthusiasms and, at fifty, was surely past the mid-life crisis – though as far as she knew he'd never gone through one. Maybe it was one of those things that, if it didn't appear at the proper time, saved itself up for later – like Muffy's toddler tantrums, which she'd expected at two, but which had manifested themselves at an embarrassingly later stage.

She wished now she had talked more to Ruth about it, but she found it difficult nowadays, even with Ruth, to discard the image she'd built up – beautiful, carefree Polly. Yet looking at Ruth's sensible round face and wispy hair across the table at lunch, it had seemed to her that Ruth, for all her husband's lack of success and her son's shiftlessness, had somehow rather more control over her life than she, perfect Polly, would ever have. She brushed the thought aside.

There was a soft knock on the door, and Sandra, tall and unsmiling, appeared discreetly round it. 'I've brought you a cup of tea, Mrs Lonsdale.'

'Mmm. Just what I need.' The cup was brought across the room to Polly, and she sipped appreciatively. 'Any visitors? Any calls?'

'Yes, Mrs Lonsdale, one for Mr Lonsdale about a meeting next week. And a French bank rang; I've left a note for him.' Among her other abilities, Sandra spoke irritatingly good French. 'And Jessica will be a bit late. I put your coat upstairs, by the way.'

Was there a note of reproach in her voice? Polly looked up in mild surprise at the familiar lanky figure with its unstylish ponytail, its over-bright jumper and skirt. Sandra was not only devoted to the girls – she had been hired as a nanny when Muffy was born, and stayed on – but also, Polly was sure, to herself. They had a kind of casual intimacy that was very comfortable: she would chat with Sandra when she had the time, borrow cash when she had none to hand, pass on once-worn clothes – that sort of thing.

Sandra was a Baptist; she'd made an inexplicable conversion to what Polly considered perhaps the least glamorous form of Christian faith years back. Polly suddenly wondered whether she could throw any light on Edward's new people; so far, Sandra had kept a discreet silence about the strangers who disappeared into Edward's study. She opened her mouth to ask – and found that, oddly, the words wouldn't come.

'If you could get my things ready,' she said instead. 'You know we're off tomorrow morning?'

Already, as Sandra silently withdrew, she could see in her mind's eye the road to beloved Cottenham unfolding before her.

Polly adored Cottenham; she loved the irregular rooms with their wide, uneven boards, the cool stone flags downstairs, the main hall, the view out through the tiny panes of the upper windows across the woods in the direction of the sea. The main building was listed, of course, and almost perfect; mercifully Edward's family had been too poor in the eighteenth century to add a fashionable new front, and a few decades later the Jacobean façade was regarded as something of a curiosity, so the Victorians had contented themselves with adding a sizable Gothic wing. For the most part Polly had left the house just as it was, and simply added a few extra bathrooms, a new kitchen and, with Ruth, had lovingly planned colour schemes, paper, paint.

There were large grounds, too – almost a park – surrounded by an ancient wall. There were outbuildings and two farms, which were managed by Edward's brother Toby. Concentrating on the garden, Polly had become something of an expert; her roses, her huge herbaceous border, were her great pride, and the restoration of the box-edged formal garden to the west of the house. Before Cottenham, brought up in the suburbia of the Thames valley, she'd always been alarmed by real country; cold and uninteresting, worth a glance, or useful as a backdrop to the drama of her life, no more. Now she loved it passionately.

To the children Cottenham was heaven; to Edward it was not only home, but extremely useful for entertaining, for there were enough spare bedrooms for a number of guests. With a slightly sinking heart, Polly had gone along with this; it was not a natural talent of hers, but with all the help she had, it was no problem – though Edward's business colleagues were something of an endurance test. He would shoot and sail with the sportier ones, and Woodbridge, with its antique and craft shops, was a happy browsing ground for other visitors. There was a good local pub for snack lunches, and enough congenial neighbours to enliven Saturday dinner parties. Polly had, after all, opted for the life she led – she would keep her part of the bargain.

This weekend, rarely, it would be just the family – with guests for Sunday lunch and a drinks party to go to the evening before. Maybe she'd have a chance to ask Edward about the Christians, and to try and have a proper talk with Jessica.

CHAPTER 2

Polly put her feet up on the sofa; she had about an hour before Edward came back, and she must tidy herself up before he did; he liked her to look her best. She forced herself to dwell on Jessica and her problems.

From those early days, no one – and she had done the rounds – had been able to identify quite what was wrong. The first sign had been the terrifying fits; the tiny body would arch in fearful spasms for minutes at a time, after which, blessedly, the child would fall into a deep sleep. Initially they'd said mild brain damage; then, when it became fashionable, autism – then they'd doubted that, the classic symptoms were missing. All the specialists could finally agree on was that, apart from the constantly adjusted drugs they gave her, there was nothing to be done. Between the fits, Jessica was strangely distant: her beautiful clear eyes reflected an inaccessible inner world; after her first few words, well past the normal age, she spoke little and refused outside contact, preferring to sit quietly with her dolly, a vacant smile on her face.

Oh, the endless check-ups, the sessions with behaviourists, psychiatrists, even a geneticist! But the fits, controlled by the drugs, became more and more infrequent; as her boisterous peers themselves sank into the torpor of adolescence, Jessica's differences seemed less marked – she'd emerged beautiful, smiling, and largely silent. But what now? Felicity, Jess's grandmother, with whom they kept in regular touch, had no anxieties about her; but it made Polly uneasy to have to admit that, at nineteen, her older daughter was still a mystery to her. She could certainly count, read and write, but what more she might be capable of was hard to judge since she was so firmly disinclined for speech. The physiotherapy course had seemed a good idea . . . And she obviously had enough communication skills to attract Robert, even if Robert, as a potential son-in-law – a bit of a chinless wonder, she and Edward had agreed – left something to be desired. And was marriage really going to happen? Could Jessica run a house, manage children?

Thinking about Jessica and her problems always made Polly feel guilty. Deep down, she still suspected that Jessica's difficulties were all her fault. Jess was the child of her first, disastrous marriage – perhaps the nightmare of the late months of pregnancy had somehow impressed itself on the baby's developing brain. Then (and Polly never let the thought into her conscious mind), without Jessica she could have put the whole thing behind her, started again. Released, first from her possessive mother and the gentility of the little house near Henley, then from the ghastly mistake Piers' good looks and famous family had led her into, she could have had London at her feet – her playground, her stage. The pavements, always sunny in her memory, had jostled with pretty girls, no younger than herself and certainly no prettier; they lingered on the benches of fashionable pubs, they partied, carefree, late into the night.

But for Polly and her pushchair the pubs and parties had meant massive organisation and oppressive guilt; unreliable babysitters, uncomprehending au pairs whose selfishness had surpassed even her own, gave little relief in a distant world where mothers, on the whole, stayed at home. The newly rescued squares and terraces of Islington and Camden Town had been habitatted, colonised by this army of be-shifted, be-smocked complacent wives, cropped hair shiny about their calm faces or smooth down their backs – no smoother or shinier than Polly's as she left her Notting Hill flat each morning to begin a day racing from job to job.

Polly's face and figure were so clearly her fortune that it had seemed pointless not to exploit them; as a model she was on her way to fame, and she'd even started to make real money. There had been none from Piers – 'I'm sorry, Polly, I need every penny for the restaurant' – so she and Jessica were on their own. She had loved the little girl with a deep, painful love, and during the weekends when Jessica went to stay with 'bead Granny' in the country would wander forlornly round her empty flat. 'Bead Granny' – which was what Jess called Piers' mother – was one of those things she occasionally came out with that seemed to set medical opinion about her feeble-mindedness on its head. As a name for the wife of Britain's most famous living sculptor it could sound almost like lese-majesty, but in fact it was wonderfully appropriate; Felicity Broadbridge had been a great beauty in her youth, and still wore the shawls, necklaces, Indian scarves and long skirts that had suited her in her heyday – and which were becoming vernacular again by the time Jessica was aware of the language of appearance.

And that awareness had come early; some of the happiest hours Polly and Jessica spent together centred on the rituals dedicated to Polly's looks. Pluck eyebrows, wax legs, put on face mask; hours on the hair, and then of course the actual make-up, equipment carefully laid out under the brightly lit mirror as Polly applied foundation, blusher, eyeshadow, eyeliner, mascara with detached skill, her oblong grey eyes mirrored in Jessica's identical pair as the little girl sat on her throne, the bed, watching. Then ringing phone, ringing doorbell, the taxi waiting downstairs.

But the exhaustion of those days – smiling and posing all morning, a drink maybe at lunchtime (for contacts had to be maintained), the rush to the special nursery to fetch Jessica home to the untidy flat and the possible non-appearance of the babysitter – for was Polly to stay in every evening? Dress and make up yet again – and, often well after midnight, back to the flat, alone or otherwise.

It was after such an evening that Polly had met both Ruth and Edward for the first time. She'd been out – goodness knows who with, she'd forgotten half their names by this time, but there'd been dinner and dancing at the Cavalry Club, and now the two of them had the night ahead. While he waited outside for the departure of the babysitter, she let herself into the house; she was just pulling the key from the front door lock when she heard her own, first-floor door open and from the turn of the stair saw Mrs Foster's face, surrounded by wild henna'd hair, peering out.

'Glad you're back. Jessica's ever so hot. She's been crying for you. I got the doctor – he'll call back tomorrow.'

By this time they were in Jessica's tiny bedroom, where she lay under a single sheet, clear of the usual litter of teddies and books. Her normally pale face was a deep shade of pink, her greyish-blonde hair streaky on the pillow. Her left hand clutched a scarf of her mother's. Her eyes were shut.

Tears had filled Polly's own eyes as she bent over her. 'What time is the doctor coming?'

'Around ten, he said.'

Combined with her worry about Jess was the awful thought that she was meant to be working in Brighton the next day. 'Mrs Foster – Margaret – ' she always forgot that she was meant to call this formidable woman by her first name ' – I know this sounds awful, but could you possibly come tomorrow? I've got to work.'

'Sorry, Mrs Broadbridge, I've got a job on myself.'

So she'd not only shocked Mrs Foster by her unmaternal behaviour, she still had tomorrow to sort out. At that moment her escort had appeared – she must have left the front door open. 'Couldn't make out what was keeping you. No problems, I hope.' He looked furious.

'Jess isn't well.'

'Jess? Oh, your daughter. Anything I can do?'

He looked as anxious to get away as she was to get rid of him, but unfortunately Mrs Foster was by now rather enjoying herself – she was clearly fixing the scene in her mind to relate to her cronies – and it was some minutes before Polly had been able to shut the door on them and get back to Jess. My poor little girl, she thought.

She had had to cancel the next day's booking – word of her unreliability, hence undesirability, would probably get around, too. Even the day after that, Jess was certainly not well enough for her nursery, so in desperation Polly had taken her along to the photographic session – evening dresses – in a large, luxuriously furnished house in Holland Park. Apparently the owner was stepping out with the fashion editor who had commissioned the pictures – or so the gossipy photographer told Polly.

Jessica sat stoically on a huge brocade sofa with Polly beside her while they broke for half an hour. Polly, exhausted, slept briefly, and woke to see a rather dirty hand proffering a halved Kit-Kat bar to Jessica (not really allowed sweets) and herself (dieting, as usual). They took it, gratefully.

'You must be worn out,' said the owner of the hand. Polly looked up at sympathetic brown eyes, the plump face and figure. 'I'm only arranging the backgrounds, and I'm done in. Is that your little girl? She's just like you, isn't she? Show me your book – what a big doggy!'

'I had to bring her, she's not well,' Polly said defensively. Surprisingly, Jessica was holding the book out for inspection.

'She doesn't look too good. Listen, why don't we put her to bed? There's a big nursery upstairs.'

'Won't they mind?'

'Won't know.' She bent down to Jessica again. 'Would you like to go upstairs and see a real rocking horse? Mummy will be near.' She turned to Polly. 'My name's Ruth, by the way. I'll keep an eye on her – I've really done my bit, unless anything else falls over.'

After her initial fierce surprise, Polly had felt tears in her eyes, tears of gratitude that someone, anyone, was taking over. They climbed the wide staircase, Ruth carrying Jessica, and settled her down in a dusty cot under a rather threatening frieze of hobgoblins and anorexic fairies.

What seemed like hours later – they had to stay for drinks with the owner of the house, and Polly had thought how distinguished he looked with his young white hair – Ruth took Polly and sleeping Jessica home in her littered Mini.

'You mean you don't drive? Isn't that a nuisance?'

'It is, but I'm rather useless, you see.' It felt so easy to say this to Ruth, who seemed somehow to have avoided the hard-boiledness that characterised most of Polly's other fashion-world contacts.

'But haven't you got parents?'

'My father died two years ago, he was the one I got on with. My mother wanted me to move back home, but I'd go mad! Anyway, she's less keen now, she keeps telling everyone that I'm a big success – just because I made the front cover of *Vogue*. Sometimes all I want is to get out of it all – it's so awful with a child, in London! I don't know what to do for the best.'

'Someone will marry you, that's what you'll do. That man who owned the house – Lonsdale – was certainly looking you up and down. Ella was furious, I could tell.'

Seven o'clock! Flinging memories aside, Polly jumped off the sofa and ran into the hall, calling to Sandra. Sandra appeared with, Polly thought, a rather exaggerated expression of patience on her face. Sometimes she was almost too good to be true.

'How's dinner, Sandra? I'm just going upstairs to change. If you could put the drinks through in the drawing-room . . .' Darling Edward liked everything to be properly done. Usually things went smoothly. Sandra shopped, unless it was fun things, and got everything ready; Polly would then cook, and leave Sandra to sort out the other bits and pieces. For grand dinners, she called on a couple of girls to come and do the work.

'Everything's all right; the smoked salmon looked a bit odd, so I got some vichyssoise out of the freezer instead.'

'Good. I'm not surprised about the salmon – Edward was sent it by those Scottish timber people of his. Well, we can eat a bit later than usual, I bet Jessica won't be here for ages.' She suddenly noticed Sandra's brightly made-up face and her flowered turquoise two-piece – her 'best' outfit of the moment. These almost always signified that she was going on one of her outings with her fellow Baptists. 'You're not going out, Sandra, are you?'

'Oh no, Mrs Lonsdale. Certainly not.'

Upstairs in her bedroom, Polly changed – no time for a bath now. The room still delighted her, for with Ruth's help she had planned it in every shade of blue – a soft, inky carpet, chintz curtains and bedcover with a huge lace shawl thrown over it, blue stippled walls and matching bathroom beyond. A large Chinese vase held a bunch of peacock feathers which Muffy had given her, and her grandmother's enamel hairbrushes were arranged on the Regency side-table where she pretended to make up – though in fact the real work was done under the brighter lights around the bathroom mirror.

Looking into this now, Polly reflected dispassionately that she'd held up well for her thirty-eight years. Her body, exercised and massaged, was as good as ever. In her naturally silver-blonde hair the first grey streaks simply did not show; her bone structure, her long grey eyes, were still perfect, and a few discreet tucks in a few years' time would sort out any wrinkles.

She changed quickly into a rather low-cut cream silk jersey dress that Edward liked, added a gold necklace and took it off, added giant pearl earrings and a good spray of 'Byzance'. One look upstairs to see that Jessica's room was ready for her, a shout to Muffy (no response), and she was downstairs, just as she heard Edward's unmistakable key in the lock.

Another man followed him in. She stepped forward to kiss Edward and to wait for his habitual gesture; he always held her a little away from him to inspect her, his prize possession, before giving her a second kiss. But now, instead, he turned away to his companion. As the man stepped into the light from the brass chandelier, Polly was certain she had seen those close-set blue eyes, that rather too square jaw, very recently. Where?

Edward was introducing him. 'Jim, this is Polly, my wife. Polly, Jim Drogue. I do hope you don't mind if he stays for dinner.'

CHAPTER 3

Later, Polly looked back on the evening as one of the longest she'd ever endured – out of the many misspent hours in that time before she had married Edward, and some since. It wasn't that she'd actually been bored; that wouldn't have been a problem, for she'd learnt to cope early with boredom, there were tricks which had seen her through dozens of heavy dinner parties.

No, she just didn't know how to react to Jim Drogue. She'd fairly quickly identified him as the cover boy from *Christian Businessman* – but beyond that, he was unfathomable. After his greeting – a rather lengthy squeeze of her hand, a longer, sincere look into her eyes – he'd declined the use of their cloakroom – Polly had a feeling that he was a little uncertain as to what was being offered – and she'd led him through into the drawing-room.

Edward joined them; she poured him his usual dry martini, which he set down beside him. He must have had a difficult day; she was only surprised that, on top of whatever had been happening, he'd brought this stranger home.

She offered Drogue a drink. 'I'm so sorry – would you like the same, or sherry?' Some memory told her that that was what you gave to clergymen. She supposed he was one. 'Or we've got vodka, or campari – or would you like anything else?'

'No, thank you – do you have any juice? And please call me Jim, Polly – I feel as if I know you already.'

And so he might, the way he was staring at her front. She wished she'd worn her bra – the room was a little cool, in spite of the lifelike gas-fired coals cunningly arranged in the marble fireplace, and she knew her nipples were showing through her dress. She tried to catch Edward's eye, but he was watching his visitor rather tensely. Oh well, she'd just have to manage this by herself. She hoped Muffy would come down soon, at least that would be a diversion; please God she'd change out of those ripped jeans.

She arranged herself on an upright chair so that not too much leg was showing – her bosom seemed to be causing quite enough of a stir – and rapidly considered how to set the conversational ball rolling. Should she refer to the cover picture? No, Edward seemed to be in a mood which might well not be improved by the thought of her even peeping at his mail.

'So you're visiting London?'

Drogue solemnly inclined his head. 'In a manner of speaking, yes.' His accent was vaguely transatlantic. 'That is to say, we're setting up a base in the capital. Now you may want a little more information on this enterprise.'

There was a clatter outside, and Muffy stood in the doorway. Polly caught her breath.

Muffy was a tall girl, and skinny, with square, bony shoulders and large, handsome hands and feet. She had dark, absolutely straight hair, a band of freckles over her nose, and bright hazel eyes that were almost yellow. Since she considered her appearance just one more of the crosses she had to bear, she always dressed in complete disregard of it – and tonight she had gone to town. Her hair was gathered up on top of her head with what appeared to be most of the haberdashery from Mr Hibbert's, the village shop at Cottenham – ribbons, tufts of wool, sparkling pins and combs. She wore a T-shirt printed with the legend 'Wide boys do it all over', and a lime-green skirt that covered the top inch or two of fish-net tights – which culminated in red socks and industrial boots. Over it all, a burgundy brass-buttoned blazer, still dangling its swing ticket, carried a rampant emblem picked out in yellow on what would have been a breast pocket had Muffy not been more or less flat-chested.

'It fits. Clever Mum.' She twirled around, displaying more of the new school blazer, the tights, and a half-undone zip at the back of the skirt. 'But just think, you've got to mark them all!'

Better not to comment on the more striking points of the outfit, it would only draw attention to it. 'I'm so glad the things fit all right. Sandra will do the nametapes. Come and meet Mr Drogue, darling.'

Even before Muffy was perched on the arm of her father's chair, glass in hand, Drogue was continuing: 'You were asking about our long-term plans, Polly.' He cleared his throat. 'Fundamentally, we are a broadly based Christian organisation: we have decided, after much prayer, to structure ourselves quite formally, and I'm honoured to say that I have been appointed acting director. We see a big need in this country, and in the USA, from which our mission emanates, for a Christian revival at all levels. Here, moral disintegration is typified by the option for abortion, corruption in places both high and low, the great growth of interest in Satanism; these are all abhorrent to the Lord, and must be rooted out.'

Polly leant forward to see if she could detect a mad gleam in his eye – something of a mistake, as the front of her dress arrested his attention once more. Again she looked towards Edward, but he was poised with the kind of rapt attention he only gave to world-class authority figures: the superior of Muffy's convent, his accountant, the man from Dyno-Rod.

But there was more bustle in the hall; from the nature of the sounds Polly realised that Jessica had arrived, and excused herself, with some relief, to go and greet her elder daughter.

Jessica stood in the hall, as usual smiling, silent, and beautiful. Even her ghastly clothes, Polly thought – the sort of thing Robert liked to see her in, wool polo-neck, ribbed tights, corduroy skirt, and all in sharp browns and olives – could not dim her flower-like beauty. 'Jess!' she cried, and hugged her, and felt again the familiar mixture of love, pity and irritation.

Astonishingly, Jess spoke. 'I've brought Robert's dog with me. She's in the car.'

Rosie, Robert's idiotic labrador, was all she needed, Polly thought, to make the evening really sparkle. But Jess was fond of her, as she was of all animals, so she suppressed her annoyance and said, 'Well, she'll have to stay there for the time being, darling, we've got a visitor. We'll bring her in after dinner. Look, why don't you go upstairs and tidy up – no need to change – and then come in and join us.'

When Jess was ready they all went through into the dining-room, where the candles, lit by Sandra, glinted on the ornate family silver. The cold soup was already at their places, prettily decorated with chopped chives and a dash of cream. Edward looked expectantly at Drogue, who cleared his throat again.

'Would you mind if we shared a brief moment of prayer? I personally would like to thank the Lord that we have this opportunity to break bread and to share fellowship together.' He launched fluently into a detailed prayer that demanded God's blessing on most aspects of their lives, while the family crouched awkwardly, spoons at half-mast.

When this was over, and after a few routine queries from Edward to Jessica, Polly realised that she must ask Drogue to continue his saga before he did so uninvited.

'Yes,' he went on, 'we believe not just in addressing ordinary folk – the man in the Clapham omnibus, I think you say,' – Polly caught a snigger from Muffy – 'we also have an agenda to work the Lord's will through those He has called to lead.'

It was easy to distinguish Drogue's references to the Almighty; the initial letter of the pronoun was aspirated with a downward movement of the jaw which emphasised not only the significance of the Deity but an accent (mid-Western? further south?) which Polly, for all her quite serious addiction to American films, couldn't identify.

'What part of the USA do you come from?' she asked politely, or as politely as she could without addressing him by name. 'Mr Drogue' was out, at his request, and no way was she going to call him 'Jim'. She would just have to manage, as she had for years with Edward's stepmother, who'd wanted the next generation, impossibly, to call her 'Grumsy'.

Edward shot her a black look – clearly she'd interrupted out of turn – but Drogue smiled.

'My people are very dear to me, Polly – I have been greatly blessed in them, and I hope I will be granted the opportunity of bringing you together with my wife Charlene before too long.'

Can't be long enough for me, thought Polly. 'But I feel we are at this moment guided to talk of my plans, or, I should say, of God's plans manifested in our movement, "The Followers" – the reasons for our choice of this name will of course be clear to you. As I was saying, we wish to approach the leadership of your fine country for their support in the furtherance of our aims.' Well, Polly thought, at least he's dropped the pretence that they're to do with God. 'I have already been able, through God's grace – ' there he went again ' – to secure a number of introductions in high places; in fact I think I can say that – praise the Lord – we are within reach of making contact with a certain member of your royal family, whom the Lord has blessed with the spark of His word.'

Polly was momentarily past speech. She looked round the table. Edward, his handsome white head slightly on one side, was looking at Drogue with the proud, enquiring expression of a mother at her child's dancing class. Jessica, her pale cheeks slightly flushed, was attending to the last of her plateful. But Muffy's skinny shoulders were heaving, what could be seen of her face was scarlet – the rest was covered by a napkin which she held against her mouth. From behind it came strange choking noises. She caught her mother's eye, at which only the caution Polly had learned, her fear of a real family scene, made it possible for her to suppress her own giggles. But her voice was shaking as she said: 'Muffy, why don't you go and ask Sandra if there's any of the chicken left? We could have a second helping.' Somehow she'd got to prevent Muffy's outburst – even the prolongation of this meal was worth it. Muffy tottered to the door – outside there was a loud howling sound which diminished as she made her way to the kitchen.

'Is your daughter – I'm sorry, I didn't quite catch her name – is she quite well, Polly?'

'She's called Muffy. She'll be fine. You know what these girls are like.'

'Yes,' Drogue replied, 'I would like to say I'm sensitive to the needs of this age group – those, of course, who we feel are in a position to go forward as leaders in life. One of my own publications, *Winners for Christ*, was in fact written specifically to encourage teenagers in active faith. We have a number of young people in our movement – we are forming an integrated division for them, which your daughter might care to join. Sometimes the young, these Christians-to-be, do behave a little strangely – quite often this heralds a very special entry of the Spirit into their lives.' Polly prayed to anyone up there not currently occupied with Drogue's organisation that Muffy would stay outside just a little bit longer. 'For this very reason we are developing a team of experienced counsellors for the guidance and enablement of our younger folk.'

At this point Muffy re-entered, under control, though still as red as a beetroot.

'Muffy,' said Drogue, 'you have a very strange name, if I may say so.'

Edward spoke. 'We christened her Cordelia, actually; she called herself Muffy from the start.' He sounded rather apologetic.

'Cordelia, too, is a little unusual.'

'Could be worse,' said Jessica suddenly, 'could be Goneril, or Regan.' Polly, amazed, dropped her fork with a clatter.

'That would be you, big sister!' said Muffy. The two girls grinned at each other.

Drogue gave them a puzzled look and carried on. 'In The Followers, with all respect,' he glanced at Edward, 'we take the names of our members very seriously. Many of those who join us, even though they have already been baptised, have a name that is some way from being truly Christian. We find that most of our members, or disciples, prefer to celebrate their rebirth in the Spirit by taking a name with a wholly Biblical precedent – a fresh name for a new life.'

Then how about Charlene? Polly just prevented herself from asking, but her tact was to no avail; Muffy had already stepped in. 'You mean, like Catholic converts?'

Drogue had just been spooning in a mouthful of the excellent lemon meringue pie which had followed the chicken. When Muffy spoke he swallowed, choked, and turned an even more alarming shade of red than she had been. The women of the family set to with glasses of water and well-placed pats on his back – in Polly's case rather harder than they need have been.

He soon recovered, and as she saw them through to the drawing-room, she heard Edward's aside to his daughter: 'Muffy, the Followers don't identify very strongly with Roman Catholic beliefs.' She also caught Muffy's look of bewilderment.

CHAPTER 4

After that, things relaxed a little. Drogue was speechless for a while. Polly poured the coffee, and told them about her visit to the Norwegian pictures that morning.

'It was a real treat, just enough to have a good look and not get tired of them. There were a few dreadful ones of characterful fisherfolk, that sort of thing, but the landscapes were superb. The light is so different, so beautiful. I wanted to go there straightaway!'

'We will go,' said Edward.

'Oh, I'd love to. The Sondersholms were the best – we saw a couple in Paris, Edward, do you remember; there were half a dozen big oils, and some drawings. You could see how passionate he was about the light; of course he was, only having daylight for half the year, poor thing. Then he'd done a couple of winter ones, gloomy interiors.'

Polly stopped abruptly as her eye travelled round the walls. Part of Edward's inheritance had been a sizable number of turn-of-the-century oils dutifully collected by his grandfather. Lavishly detailed, richly coloured, each told a story, or part of a story. Polly, after her initial horror, had become quite fond of them. The best two hung in the alcoves on either side of the fire. In one, a serving-wench, a hand to her bosom, stood at the door of a candlelit room, the recipient of an unambiguous leer from a red-robed cardinal. In one hand she held an opened letter. But would she be literate, in whenever it was supposed to be? Polly had always wondered. Was the letter from the cardinal, and if so, why, when they clearly had every opportunity for intercourse of every kind? In the other painting, two more princes of the church, glasses at their elbows, were at a game of cards – one smiled approvingly at his lapdog, who was pulling a rival trump off the table.

Alien as these were to modern taste, Polly, to the fury of her newly married husband, had had them reframed; and unfortunately the original frames, which had carried fairly lengthy descriptive material, were now mislaid somewhere in the attics, so the clue to the pictures' content was lost. But what would Drogue make of them if he didn't approve of Catholics? Unfortunately her glance had drawn his eye to them, but his face told her nothing.

Polly herself was perplexed by his attitude. Although she was not a Catholic, her mother had approved of convent education – cheap; nice class of girl – and had managed to place her with the local sisters. There, until the money ran out again and her mother had to take her away, Polly had been blissfully happy, taking on board such rather sporadic education as the nuns saw fit to give her, lustily singing Catholic versions of pirated Protestant hymns, and spending many hours on her knees in front of a blue-robed statue of Our Lady. The nuns, gentle or otherwise, had taught her to love the paraphernalia of their faith, and she still kept a rosary in her bedside drawer.

So what was wrong with Catholics, that Drogue shouldn't approve of them? Of course there had been the Inquisition, and the terrible zeal of the missions to South America, but that was a while ago. The Masses she had attended with Muffy at her convent were a world away from what she remembered in her own day; held in the local church, they had seemed delightfully laid-back, with toddlers running up and down the aisles and people coming and going, just like a supermarket. They were all fellow Christians, anyway – if Drogue felt so badly about them, how would he react to Moslems, or Jews? She wanted to ask, but he'd be there all night! She'd get Edward to explain; it would be a good way of finding out more about these Followers.

Edward, meanwhile, was promising Muffy he'd take her to the Scandinavian exhibition before the holidays were over. It then transpired that Drogue's mother's parents had left Norway for the States in the early part of the century – on their reasons for doing so, and on his own memories of his visits to their wooden house in a Norwegian-speaking community in Illinois, he was, though still incapable of dialogue, far more interesting than on the subject of the Followers. The years had certainly drawn a veil over the bad bits, thought Polly, but it did sound idyllic; blueberry-picking expeditions, rides in the hay cart, the ample simplicity of family meals as they gathered in the huge whitewashed kitchen. Even Muffy was listening, and Jessica looked spellbound. Unfortunately it was impossible to keep Drogue off-track for long.

'Although I owe a great debt to my dear mother, may the Lord bless her, it was truly in the home of my grandparents that I took my first steps towards Jesus – ' But just as he was fairly launched again, the doorbell rang. It was a neighbour; the Labrador was apparently going mad in the car outside.

An expression of pain crossed Jessica's face. 'Oh, poor Rosie, I forgot about her. I'll take her round the square.'

Polly looked covertly at the nineteenth-century ormolu clock on the mantelpiece – too revealing to consult her own tiny gold watch. Eleven thirty, and high time Muffy was in bed, let alone herself. Blessedly, Edward caught her glance – he rose, and the goodbyes began.

'It was gracious of you to welcome me into your home, Polly; I have truly appreciated meeting you. I shall hope we can talk again soon, and may the Lord bless you until that time. You too, Milly.' He turned a special smile on Muffy. 'Goodbye, Edward; I shall look forward to our dialogue tomorrow.'

Jessica moved towards the door.

'Jessica,' Drogue said, 'if it would not inconvenience you, I would be happy to accompany you on your walk. Although I'm not from the South, I still believe in some of those old-fashioned courtesies – and I would very much like to talk further with you.'

'All right,' said Jessica, pulling on her sheepskin. Her face was expressionless.

'Have you got a key, Jess?'

Jess nodded at her father. In fact Edward would have to come down anyway, to set their elaborate burglar alarm.

With a few more blessings, the door slammed on them. Polly

sank onto the chair in the hall. She kicked off her shoes and looked up at Edward, who was leafing through his post. 'That lot can wait till morning,' he said. 'What did you think of him? He's got some interesting ideas, hasn't he?' He wasn't quite meeting her eyes. 'He can be a bit heavy, I know. I'm thinking of working quite closely with this group of his.'

Her stomach gave a small lurch. 'What on earth do you mean?'

He turned to look at her. His handsome features had taken on an expression of earnestness she had not seen before. 'Look, Polly, I know you're not in sympathy with Christianity at present, though I have a real feeling that that will change. Just think of this as a moral revival he's trying to get going, and even you must be aware how badly that's needed.'

'What's all this, "even me"?'

'I'm sorry, Polly, I don't want to sound hostile. But the whole country's in a bad way: top businessmen lie and cheat, there are frightful scandals in local government; the whole system's breaking down – you've only got to look at football violence, those prison riots, to see what he's trying to alter. Then there's the breakdown of the family; divorce up by around thirty per cent in the last five years, truancy, young things running wild.' He seemed to come down to earth rather sharply. 'I could have done without Muffy's outfit this evening, by the way.'

Polly shrugged. 'It doesn't mean anything – they all go round like that.'

'That's part of the problem; this herd instinct. But there are worse things – Satanism really is taking a hold – you've read about ritual child abuse, it's only becoming apparent now how widespread it is, and what's behind it.'

Polly felt her jaw drop. He had never talked like this before. 'You don't really believe all that, do you?' she said. 'The police don't. A bunch of hysterical social workers, if you ask me – and the kids watching too many videos.' What had got into him?

'Whatever you think, there have to be changes. The fact that Jim wants to make them through something you don't believe in doesn't alter the facts. I'm certain he's right in wanting to go to the top – and that's where he thinks I can help him.'

He was serious. No good arguing – it never was when Edward had made up his mind about something. She tried another tack. 'Edward, I still don't see how. I know you've got a lot of contacts in the City and around, but if he's already onto the Royals we're not going to be much use, are we? Presumably he'd know all our sort of people already, and I must say I don't think many of them would be interested. Anyway, you can't alter great groups of people like that.'

'Well, we think you can. Jim – and you could have called him by his Christian name when he asked you to, Polly – he wants me as the co-ordinator for his work.'

'Look, don't let's quarrel,' said Polly. She went up to him. 'We're both tired, and you can tell me more over the weekend. Meanwhile, talking of morals, what's he doing with my daughter out in the square?'

In fact this was the cue for Jessica to come back in, Rosie straining on her lead. 'Put her downstairs in the back room,' Polly said. 'Have you got her rug? And do shut her in or she'll be all over the house, like last time.'

When they were alone again, Edward put his arms round Polly and rested his head on her shoulder; she still found his familiar physical presence disturbing. The evening went out of her mind as he kissed her. Still linked, they walked upstairs to the bedroom, where Sandra had turned down the covers. By the time Edward returned from the dressing-room Polly was in bed in ice-blue satin and lace, pretending to look at *Harpers*. But Edward, after another rather paternal kiss, turned away from her and reached for his book.

This had happened often lately – in fact Polly could hardly remember the last time they'd made love – after Edward came back from his trip to Hong Kong, was it? Perhaps the Christians were against it; she was certain this whole business had something to do with it. She'd never discussed sex with Edward, no need. There'd been no problems till now. It was hardly the moment to start talking about it.

Edward finished reading and put his light out. She lay there, wakeful; then, when he was asleep, she got up and went out onto the landing. She could hear Jessica above; she walked upstairs.

'Did you get Rosie tucked away safely?'

Jessica smiled her sensational smile.

'And did you see Jim Drogue off all right?' She didn't want to seem like a prying mother, but she did long to find out what had passed between them.

Again the lovely smile, and then Jessica turned away, switching on her bedside lamp and getting her nightdress out from under her pillow.

Knowing herself dismissed, Polly left the room and wandered downstairs. There was light under Muffy's door; she should be asleep by now, but Polly felt too restless to resist the chance of a chat.

Muffy was in bed, oddly propped up on her pillows and looking through one of the family photograph albums. Her head was gleaming with metal.

'Muffy, what have you got in your hair?'

'They're the proper clips for doing Marcel waves – I'm going all Thirties tomorrow. I found them in a box at Mr Hibbert's and bought the lot. I should flog the rest to those idiots who do hair in films – you know how they always get it wrong.'

'I remember – your granny had some. But aren't they agony? Will you sleep a wink? And why the fuss?'

'I'm hoping Harry will take me across to The Gunnocks tomorrow, to see the murals they're having in the hall. I saw a photo of the chap who's doing them in one of the Sundays. He's gorgeous. I know he'll fall for my hair!'

'Well, he wouldn't right now!' Polly smiled quizzically down at her daughter. 'No mischief, mind, Muffy.'

'Nonsense, Mum, how could you! You know I'm still in love with Dave, even though an ocean separates us. Talking of love, what was Jess up to in the square with that man? Suppose I tell Robert – you know how jealous he is!'

'You dare! No, I asked her, but she didn't say a thing. By the way, did you have to make such a show of yourself, laughing at him like that? He was a bit much, though, wasn't he?' For a moment she felt like giggling – but only a moment. 'He was fine when he wasn't going on about God – but your father seems to be rather into all that. I was a bit alarmed by all this talk of setting up a large-scale organisation; I just hope Edward doesn't give him too much money.' Polly waited; often, Muffy knew better than she did what was going on.

But Muffy only laughed. 'He won't, Mum. Anyway, you could always sell your snuffboxes.' She settled herself more comfortably against her pillows. 'So you didn't find out if he made a pass at Jess?' This happened quite a lot to Jessica, whose beauty was enhanced by her remoteness, her air of helplessness. She never appeared to notice. 'You should have sent me up to ask her about it, Mother, I'm a better interrogator than you are. Anyway, I can tell you what they were talking about on the sofa: this book he's writing – study, he called it – on Revelations. Then he was carrying on a treat about what a meaningful partnership he and Charlene have – that always makes you wonder, doesn't it? Usually it's divorce ten minutes later.'

How acute she was! 'I'm sure it's all above board – anyway, Jessica's hardly going to run off with him.'

'Don't be too sure, Mum, you know what they say about the allure of the older man and all that. Not my type, I have to say, terminal boredom, but quite attractive in that clean-cut way.' She yawned. 'Go to bed, Mum, Jessica will be all right.'

Polly climbed in beside Edward, and put a tentative arm round him. He stirred and muttered in his sleep. The wind was still high; her heavy curtains shifted disturbingly and she caught a glimpse of the plane tree blowing about outside, and of a crescent moon between the clouds. She was still wakeful. For a long time her life had followed a pattern which suited her so well, a safe cocoon of money and admiration. She'd never really envisaged anything different; after all, her own qualities, her looks, her adaptability, had brought her to this position, and she'd worked hard to stay there. Of course she would get older, but there were good things to come; perhaps Edward would sell the company, at any rate on his retirement there'd be lovely Cottenham and her garden; she'd see that they kept on a flat in London, and spent much more time in France. Polly adored the sun.

But now things seemed to be changing. She even felt a little insecure about Edward's feelings for her – and the celibate life they were living at the moment didn't help. Under his urbane manner he was a shy and restrained man; apart from his looks and his money, one of his greatest attractions for her had been the passion that had been roused by her and her alone: 'It's your magic,' he'd breathed the first time they made love, and this sense of possessing a unique power had put a spell on her too.

Why was the magic fading? It wasn't just Edward and this religious business; her assured place at the centre of things seemed to be vaguely threatened. Sandra's manner was noticeably odd; she had been unusually vivacious as she came and went during the evening, beaming away at Jim Drogue – but then maybe she'd met him already, Edward could perfectly well have brought him to the house before, during the day while she was out. She would ask him. Then Ruth hadn't looked too well when she saw her – she'd only really thought about it afterwards . . . Muffy, exhausting, endearing, was much the same as usual; but as for Jessica and Robert, she wasn't at all certain about this idea of marriage . . . she must go and talk to Felicity about it . . .

Still worrying, Polly finally fell asleep.

CHAPTER 5

Some time in the small hours, Polly woke up. She must have been dreaming, dreaming about Felicity: the image of Piers' mother was sharp in her mind. Not Felicity as she was now, as Polly saw her on the regular trips she made into Sussex to visit her, but Felicity as she had been the day she first met her, when Piers took her down to the Broadbridge estate for the first time, and they had come upon her quite casually, seated at her writing-desk in a cluttered sitting-room in the main farmhouse. She was busy on one of her lengthy letters to her husband, she had explained, turning gracefully to meet her son and his prospective bride. Tristram was away, working on a commission in Huddersfield.

Polly had stared at her – at the fine, aquiline nose, the slightly hyperthyroid dark eyes, the cloud of unashamedly dyed auburn curls. Felicity sat swivelled in her chair, one arm along its back. The fingers of the strong hand which rested there, still holding her pen, were covered with rings, their settings rich with stones Polly couldn't identify. In a year of clothes pared to the bone, she was wearing a full, striped skirt, green stockings, pointed velvet shoes of archaic design – red velvet, buckled – a number of necklaces and a flowered shawl. Even to Polly's inexperienced and conventional eye she had looked marvellous. Polly, who was wearing a man's shirt (Piers's) and a pink-and-white checked gingham skirt ineptly made by herself, had never felt more ill at ease.

'What a charming little outfit,' Felicity had said. 'Funny how these short skirts come and go . . . Piers, you never told me how pretty she is. But then you never tell me anything! Tristram would love to draw you, Polly dear.'

'I've drawn her, Mother,' said Piers.

'Of course, darling, you must show me.'

Polly had looked silently from one to the other of them. She was so used to seeing Piers, the most promising art student of his year, at the centre of an admiring crowd: it was strange to hear his mother addressing him as if he was a five-year-old bringing home his first effort from school.

That afternoon, Polly had been almost as fascinated by Felicity Broadbridge as she was by Piers. She was enchanted, too, by the rambling old farmhouse, the cottages and outbuildings housing Tristram's apprentices and large extended family, the barns adapted as studios and workshops. Now in his seventies, Tristram Broadbridge had long since achieved respectability and international renown, his massive pieces much in demand for important open-air sites and public buildings; but in earlier days he had been a good deal less respectable, and there had been a number of mistresses and many children, none of whom seemed ever to have left. She knew all this from Piers, of course, but it had been a different thing altogether to come and see things for herself – and to meet Felicity, who had been not only a famous beauty but a celebrated painter in her own right, until she married Tristram and diplomatically allowed his talent to eclipse hers.

No wonder, Polly thought now, smiling in the dark as she remembered, that she had worked so hard to avoid Felicity's questions about her own dreary home counties background: the awful little dress shop her mother had started up when her father died, the hideous overgrown cottage they'd had to move into at the edge of the golf course. Though amazingly, it was at the golf club that she had met Piers; he'd been brought along by some friend, and she was instantly smitten, not only by his beauty but by his look of complete bewilderment at finding himself there.

How she had loved him! Polly thought, twisting impatiently in the big bed beside the solidly sleeping Edward. How she had been besotted by that dark gold hair, those green eyes. Oh, what a silly girl she had been!

After tea, in a conservatory dense with leggy geraniums, with two of Piers' sisters – awkward, hearty girls who had obviously inherited their mother's large bones but not her good looks – Polly had helped to carry the china through to the kitchen. She was stunned by the squalor that met her eyes: two cats were quarrelling over a heap of feathers on the central table, and half-finished dishes, their contents fossilised, covered every surface and filled the huge, chipped porcelain sink. She had retreated in horror; but back in the sitting-room, her eyes suddenly opened, she saw that here, too, the charming clutter of objects was covered with a thick layer of dust – and Felicity's hands were none too clean.

Felicity had taken her aside. 'Now I'm not going to be a prying mother-in-law,' she had said, 'but I do want you to feel you can always turn to me, Polly, that you can always tell me anything you need to. You're sure about this marriage, are you?' She had looked hard at Polly, and Polly had wondered what on earth she wanted to know. She must have worked out that Polly had moved in with Piers months ago – surely she didn't expect any little confidences about this side of their lives? After a pause Felicity had continued: 'He's a wonderful boy – so talented. But he's not really like his father.' Probably a good thing, Polly had thought, at least as far as marriage is concerned.

On the way back in Piers' little sports car, he had stopped at the edge of a tall beech wood. He had put his arms round her and kissed her. Leaving the car, they had walked into the wood, and there, among the trees, they had made uncomfortable love, protected from the carpet of earth and prickly fallen leaves only by Piers' even more prickly jacket, which never seemed to be in quite the right place. After she had retrieved her pants and pulled some of the twigs from her hair, Piers had produced a small box from his pocket. 'Crichton's Worm Pills', it announced.

'I wondered what that bump was!'

'Go on, open it.' He had turned away; he was usually so in control of things, she was charmed to see him embarrassed.

'Oh Piers!' she had said when she saw what was inside, 'how pretty! I love topazes!'

'It's not a topaz, you silly, it's a brown diamond. Mother kept it always for me to give to the girl I married.'

Polly remembered the momentary stab of disappointment she had felt that he hadn't chosen it himself. But she had told herself that this was her bourgeois background surfacing again; she must adapt herself to her new life.

And, a natural chameleon, she had managed it. She had abandoned the pink check skirt and become used to living in a sea of unwashed coffee cups and discarded wine glasses; Piers would laugh good-humouredly at her attempts to tidy up. He himself had never lifted a dirty shirt off the floor in his life. He painted with some success, but sporadically, for the Belsize Park studio they rented was more often than not full of people – friends from Piers' art school days, aspiring actors, fledgling writers, all crowding in for impromptu parties that sometimes went on all night, leaving their big downstairs room dense, by morning, with smoke and the smell of pot.

She had been proud to be admitted to this magic circle, delighted to be shown off to Piers' many friends. She had quickly thrown off her inhibitions, the polite days of her mother's sherry parties ('Just a small one for me!') were far behind as she posed naked for Piers and later picked her way, smiling, through the brightly dressed couples who shared the cushions on the studio floor.

Then she got pregnant, and things changed. She had felt so ill she wanted to cry. Unable to get up, she had lain all day on the grubby sheets, her skin so sensitive all over that she couldn't bear Piers to touch her. His friends continued to come, and would pile upstairs to sit on her bed and drink and chat till all hours. Piers, now busy setting up an exhibition, would come back to find her weeping among the dirty ashtrays. He seemed happy with the idea of a baby, but bemused by the changes in her.

And then, one morning –

Polly opened her eyes wide in the darkness and stared up at the dim ceiling. This was the uncomfortable bit. It was still uncomfortable after all these years. She squeezed her eyes shut again, and let the memories come.

She had woken late one April morning to find herself alone in the bed. It hadn't worried her – Piers was probably round at the gallery again. But the marvellous thing was that she felt well. She didn't feel sick! Some crucial stage of her pregnancy was obviously over. Carefully she had got out of bed and found some clothes – noticing with interest that she could only just do up her jeans. More than anything she wanted to be outside. A little unsteadily on her bedridden legs, she had set off for Hampstead Heath.

She had never had much sense of direction, and had wandered aimlessly over the grass, the sun warm on her face. Dog walkers passed her, mothers with pushchairs – she had beamed at them all. She felt so well.

At last she had reached the top, and even she was able to work out where she was: Highgate, on its own hill, was magically clear to her left, and to the south lay London itself, tall buildings standing out in the haze, light glinting on the windows of the new office blocks. She had taken off her jacket and sat down on the grass.

She remembered how the squirrel had darted past her, and how, turning to watch it, it was then she had seen the two figures embracing in the shadows. Something was strange, and she had glanced again. Yes, it was two men; the fair-haired one had his arms round his friend's waist, one hand under his check shirt. She had turned self-consciously away, shocked, but touched at the evident tenderness of the couple. She had very much wanted to look again; but even as she resisted the temptation they had come into sight as they walked down the path together, now apart but with their hands still brushing.

One of them was Mark Jansen, one of Piers' old schoolfriends who had often been at the flat. The fair one was Piers himself.

Definitely the difficult bit, Polly thought, drawing her leg up so she could rub her cramped calf.

'But why didn't you tell me?' she had begged Piers a little later.

'How could I? It doesn't make any difference to how I feel about you, Polly. I love you.'

'You could have told me about you being like that – with men. Lots of people are. I do know something about it.'

'Polly, I'm not "like that". OK, I do love Mark in a way – I've known him always. We were at school together, you see. Our awful prep school.'

I can't ask him, she had thought, I just can't. But I must, I have to know. She hadn't been able to look at him as she spoke.

'Do you go to bed with him?'

'Yes.'

And she hadn't turned to Felicity. She had struggled on for a bit, but finally she had left, to take shelter with her mother. A man called Daniel had moved into the Belsize Park studio with Piers, and soon afterwards they had gone to Wales together to start a restaurant. That autumn Jessica was born in a hospital in High Wycombe.

Polly heaved a sigh into the darkness. Why on earth was she going through all this yet again? That time was over. She was lucky Polly now, and would go on being lucky Polly into the foreseeable future. Surely nothing could change that. And tomorrow they were going down to lovely Cottenham.

Turning over once more, Polly fell at last into a dreamless sleep, forty-five minutes before her alarm was set to go off.

CHAPTER 6

Cottenham. Cottenham in the spring. Six months had passed since that September evening when Edward had first brought Jim Drogue home to Connaught Square, and much had changed. To Polly, as she stood with Ruth looking out of the window of the big, stone-flagged kitchen at the exuberant landscape beyond, it felt as if the hysterical cries of the birds and the ephemeral beauty of the new flowers mocked her low spirits, and held a foolish unawareness of their own mortality. You'll be dead soon, she felt like shouting at the massed ranks of early daffodils as they nodded their fleshy heads in unison. Anyway, she didn't like yellow.

'Aren't they lovely?' Sandra came into the room and paused briefly but matily beside them. She was carrying great armfuls of the offending daffodils, clearly intent on arranging them in vases round the house. Sandra was tirelessly, exhaustingly cheerful these days, the ponytail jauntier, the garish clothes even brighter. Or perhaps they were just seeing too much of her; she'd been coming to Cottenham with them every weekend since Mrs Beamish had left. Somebody had to help in the house, which was increasingly full of Edward's Christians. How Polly regretted now the hearty business contacts who used to weekend here! She'd laughed about them at the time, with their new smart suitcases, their over-elaborate sporting gear; she'd cursed their unruly dogs and the sheer effort of entertaining them and their wives, carefully dressed in country clothes – but what wouldn't she give to see them back again. Several of the couples had become real friends, and at least they'd had a bit of style, which you could hardly say about the

Followers. This much Mrs Beamish had intimated as she gave her reasons for leaving; Polly had a feeling the absence of the fat tips she was used to had something to do with it. The discovery that the old girl was going to housekeep at The Gunnocks had been the last straw.

Polly gave herself a shake. Really, she must try and pull herself together – Ruth would think she had gone peculiar. 'So what's The Gunnocks like now, Ruth?' she said. 'It must be nearly finished, isn't it? I'm longing to see it.'

'Well, actually, it's rather marvellous. I've got to do a piece on it, of course, for the mag. I just hope I don't have to go back into hospital again.' Polly looked at her enquiringly: hospital? But Ruth hurried on: 'It'll be another couple of weeks, Harry says, but it's bound to take longer, it always does.'

'What, hospital? Oh, The Gunnocks. I'd love to see it – and of course we must all go to this do together. You know they're having the handicapped spring ball there? So Harry will have to have it finished by then.'

'I hope he does! We'd love to come with you.' Ruth frowned. 'But I thought you said Edward wasn't into that kind of thing any more, now he's seen the light?'

Polly directed a warning glance towards Sandra, who was now arranging some of the horrible daffodils in two horrible vases. 'Where on earth did those pots come from, Sandra?' she asked brightly. 'I've never seen them before.'

'They were a gift from Charlene, Jim's wife – she crafted them herself, and felt they would be in keeping with the spirit of our prayer room.' Sandra stood back from her handiwork for a moment, smugly admiring it. 'I'll be off, then, and leave you two to have a chat.' She left the room self-importantly, bearing the pottery jugs reverently before her.

'Bloody hell!' Polly exploded as soon as the door had closed behind her. 'Patronising old cow! "Our prayer room" indeed – they mean my drawing-room!' She paused to let her indignation subside. 'No, about the dance – Edward isn't too keen, but he feels he ought to go – after all, we always have before.'

Ruth stared at her friend thoughtfully. 'Won't it be a bit awful, though, if he's doing it out of a sense of duty? He used to love that kind of thing, too.'

'He hasn't changed entirely, you know.' Polly knew she sounded defensive. Then: 'Oh Ruth, I do so hope he'll give all this up! It's getting worse all the time. We've got eight of the Followers here now, not counting the children. There's one quite nice man – gay, I should think, though it's hard to tell; one desperate old girl, two couples, one lot really frightful, and a family – well, Mum and the two kids, they were the first here. They're all right, the kids, though they're run off their feet with all the praise and worship going on the whole time, and they're not allowed to do a thing – I heard the mother carrying on at the big one for reading one of Muffy's old *Beanos* the other day, and that was nothing to the row when Muffy took them out trick-and-treating round the village at Halloween.'

'Polly, it must drive you mad. Can't you just ask them to go? It's your house as well as his.'

'No way is it my house. I love it, I love it, but it came down through Edward's mother, you know that. It's Edward's house.' She paused. 'Not that that ever worried me before.'

'Look, why don't you just tell Edward you can't cope with these people around?'

Polly sighed wearily. 'I have, and he just looks at me. We've never really had rows, you know, so I'm not in practice. Then he explains, very patiently, that he feels that this is what is meant to be just now. I asked him if he didn't mind how I felt any more, and he said he thought it was important, but it was just a part of things. He said he thought I'd soon feel the way he does.' A bit of Polly's usual spark returned to her. 'I shouldn't think I would, not in a million years.'

'How do the girls feel about it?'

'Well, Jessica's silent as usual – she's been coming here quite a lot. She'd rather got in with this family, though I expect that will all be over after the *Beano* business. You should have heard the mother – Bethany, her name is – going on about "corruption" and "values". Honestly, Ruth, it was just the dear old *Beano*! But Jessica seems to be rather keen on Jim, the man who runs it all –

luckily he's in the States most of the time. When he's here she hangs round him, and Robert gets in a frenzy.'

Polly had the panic feeling, sometimes, that she was falling the length of a slope which it would be impossible to climb again – here a handhold slipped, there her foot gave way, and down she went. She'd always thought of herself as rather an observant person, and had delighted, at first, in noticing the quirks of behaviour, the looks, the clothes of the new people Edward brought to the house in increasing numbers – what she hadn't really taken account of was the changes in Edward and in herself. He had been as gentle and loving as ever, perhaps more so – he had, after all, been a regular attender at the tiny pseudo-Norman parish church at Cottenham, so this whole religious thing shouldn't be so much of a surprise. When she had brought herself to think about it, what really irked her was not so much that this dear, strong man, her protector, her saviour, should be under the influence of this alien creed, these alien people – above all, of Jim Drogue – but that his attention should have been so wholly diverted from herself.

She refused to think of Drogue as a real person; he was a joke figure, with ridiculous ideas and a ridiculous way of expressing them. But Edward's respect for him, the obvious efficiency with which he ran his group, the number of people – some of them socially and politically significant – who were in his thrall, did impress her against her will. She also strongly suspected that he was a crook, which gave titillating overtones to his perorations. A couple of months ago – it was the first time she'd really managed to talk to Edward in ages – she'd asked him where Drogue got all his cash.

'People give it to the Followers willingly, Polly, they think we're doing something important. We have a plan of action, you see, and part of what I'm involved in, Polly, is helping him to draw it up.'

He was actually starting to talk like Drogue now, speaking slowly and carefully and using her name a lot. 'How about all these other people who come round here, then,' she said. 'They don't look as if they could draw up a shopping list.'

'I don't think you're being quite fair, Polly – you should never underestimate what you call "ordinary people" . . .'

Polly came to with a start. Ruth was looking at her most oddly. 'Sorry, Ruth, it's on my mind, you see. I – ' There was the sound of feet and voices in the corridor. 'Help, I can hear them coming. They used to cook in the other kitchen, but they fancied my Aga – the next thing was they were all talking about "breaking bread" together. "Break" is about the word, the stuff they make is like a rock. Let's go down to the Coach and Horses – I'll give Muffy a shout. Yet another half-term, so she's around.'

'What about Harry? He's meant to be picking me up.'

'I'll tell Sandra where we're going.'

Halfway down the drive, they met some more of the Followers making their way up from the lodge. There was a white-haired woman in glasses whose broad smile faded abruptly as she saw Polly; a pale pink cardigan was stretched over her large bust, and on this lay a gigantic crucifix. She was accompanied by a lean, red-haired man in an Aran sweater and cords, and a young couple, arm in arm – the girl, also bespectacled, was pretty in a healthy, slightly buck-toothed way, the man was chubby and balding. He carried his glasses in his hand.

Polly greeted them diffidently; she'd never bothered to remember their names, though she was fairly certain the girl was Judy, and the red-haired man was definitely Adrian. But Muffy, who was composing a dossier on them to send to Francie, her bosom friend from the new school, ran forward.

'Please, stop! I do so want a picture of you all!'

The older woman opened her mouth as if to protest, then smoothed her pudding-basin haircut; Adrian took off his glasses and held in his stomach. The photo was taken, and the Followers, smiling benignly, went on up to the house.

When they were out of earshot, Ruth asked: 'Polly, if you hate having them here, why not just shout at them and get them out? It almost seems as if you're afraid of them! And why on earth do they all wear glasses?'

'All that poring over Holy Scripture, I suppose. They have these Bibles, covered in highlighter, practically falling to pieces. Mrs Beamish was horrified when she saw one. "I was brought up to respect the Good Book," she said.' Polly frowned. 'No, I can't shout at them, Edward got so cross when I did ask them to get out of the kitchen once. Anyway, it's like shouting at a mattress; they just smile sweetly and pray for you – that's the worst thing of all. I should think it's the nastiest feeling in the world, being prayed for.'

'Well, why on earth do you go on coming up here – wouldn't it be better to stay in London when they're having their weekends here?'

'London's full of them, too – the smart businessy ones. They're worse – they're like changelings, they look like normal people when they aren't. They don't have great big crosses, like Meg there; they have teeny-weeny little ones, or fish badges on their Armani lapels. And they want proper food. I got a girl in to cook this weekend, and came away. Look, there's Harry, he can give us a lift down to the pub.'

In the warm bar of the Coach and Horses, alight with winking copper and varnished oak, Polly relaxed while Muffy gave her own spirited account of the Followers, and of her sufferings, to Harry. Her preferred little downstairs bedroom was next to the old billiard room which the group had taken over for worship. The noise had driven her out – she was now installed in the attic.

'And they'll be up there next! I had to chase two of them out the other day! It was Meredith, she's the one who looks like a goat with those pale eyes, and her boyfriend – that ghastly one, Bart, in flares. They were looking for props for what they called a "worship event" – they'd even got hold of the old dining-room curtains. I can tell you I held on to them – we might need them for dresses one day, like Scarlett O'Hara.'

Harry, leaning on the bar, grinned across at her – 'It sounds as if they're everywhere!' – and Polly thought how reassuring Harry's grin always was. He wasn't much to look at – his small, elegant hands were his best feature – but she had always been fond of him, and he of her. Rather more than fond, actually; Harry had been Polly's acquisition first, soon after Jessica was born, when he'd conceived a hopeless romantic passion for her. Then she'd passed him on to Ruth – the three of them still laughed about it. 'Pretty

Polly', he used to call her. He was the sort of man you could feel safe with.

'They *are* everywhere. There's that awful Meg – she's the one with the huge bust who hates Mum. Then there's Simon – he's not too bad except he's in charge of the cash and I think he's fiddling Dad rotten – and Dean and Judy. I could try blackmail on them – Dean has a bottle of whisky hidden in the attic, I saw him up there. Adrian's in the stable flat – maddening, I just fancied taking it over. He's the sort of group leader so he likes to be by himself, except he keeps asking me over.'

'What?' Polly jumped to maternal attention. 'I hope you don't go!'

'No thanks. Then Bethany and her lot are in two bedrooms in the house. The kids are OK, but I don't think all this prayer suits them – they have nothing but these Bible books to read, so I lent them one of my old *Beano* annuals the other day, just to cheer them up.'

Harry laughed. 'It sounds too awful to think about – so why don't we make a few plans for this dance instead? The Gunnocks really is looking splendid, they'll do it beautifully. And you'll get a glimpse of the new owner – they say he's going to be there. Now, we're all going together, aren't we?'

Ruth and Polly smiled their agreement, and Muffy said: 'Mum says Francie can come, and I'm going to invite those twins from the Glebe to escort us.'

'Oh, Proctor and Gamble or whatever they're called,' said Polly. 'Well, it should be fun. Let's hope so. I could do with some fun just now.'

CHAPTER 7

On the night of the ball they were a smaller party than they would have been a year earlier – Polly now had no spare bedrooms in which to put up extra guests, and felt she couldn't hold a very grand dinner party under the watchful and disapproving eyes of the Followers. She didn't know what had passed between Edward and Adrian, the group leader, but some agreement had been made and the event had received, if not the Followers' approval, at least their grudging acceptance. She had at first thought there might be some frightful price to pay – perhaps they would have to take the whole lot with them. As Muffy pointed out, it would be well worth it just to see what they would wear. She managed to ask Edward, in a non-committal way, what the Followers' plans were that night; it appeared they were to be bussed down to London for a major evangelical gathering at Wembley.

'That's handy!' she'd said before she could stop herself, but Edward did laugh; yes, he said, it fitted in quite well. She presumed he'd be footing the bill for the jaunt – he must be keeping all of them, anyway – but she didn't enquire further, except to take advantage of his good humour and ask whether he wouldn't prefer the meeting to the ball.

'I have to admit I'd rather eat smoked salmon at The Gunnocks than sandwiches at Wembley.'

She had been delighted. 'Edward, I won't tell on you.'

*

'Thank heavens it's fine,' said Ruth, 'since they're planning to dance on the terrace.' She and Harry had come over, and Polly was leading them up to change in one of the bedrooms which had been requisitioned by the Followers. The bus and its passengers had departed an hour earlier, with the strains of a chorus of 'Jesus saves! Jesus saves!' borne in its wake.

Ruth stared as Polly opened the bedroom door. 'Well, it certainly looks a bit different in here,' she said. Bright posters were tacked up over the soft colours of the floral wallpaper; 'Christ is our King', 'Praise the Lord' and longer legends were overprinted at random on pictures of bunny rabbits, woodland scenes and flaming sunsets. A coverlet printed in orange and red had been thrown over the old patchwork quilt on the bed, and some gaily-coloured cushions arranged on the faded chintz of the chairs.

'Isn't it awful?' said Harry frankly. 'Looks as if they've really moved in, too. Edward's crazy having them here.'

Polly smiled manfully. 'I know – but at least he's coming tonight. I'll go and see how the girls are doing.'

Ready at last, they all descended and stood in the hall: Edward impeccable in his white tie, Polly in pale blue silk, fat Francie in black. Muffy's skinny shoulders emerged from a sea of silvery ruffles. Edward looked nervously at the girls' two indistinguishable escorts, usually to be seen knocking about the place in jeans and trainers; by some miracle, they were both presentable.

'Muffy, you look stupendous,' said her father, kissing her.

'Thank you so much, Pa. Oxfam, and if you hear me roaring with mad laughter, it'll be these frills – they tickle like anything. Here come Jessica and Robert. Jess, what a dress! It's a treat. Where's Rosie?'

Jess was ravishing in a dress of wispy green chiffon; Robert, with his long face, looked goofier than ever in evening dress, Polly thought. He said: 'Sandra's got Rosie shut up in the kitchen.' He cleared his throat. 'Er, Sandra doesn't seem very happy about staying this evening. I have an idea she wanted to go to Wembley with the – er – Followers.'

'Who, Sandra? Wanted to go to Wembley? Whatever for?' Polly was indignant. 'Curiosity, I suppose. Well, I like to have someone around – there were two burglaries in the village last month.'

There was a little silence, and then, to Polly's amazement, Jessica said solemnly: 'Mum, sometimes I feel you rather use Sandra.'

'Not at all, she loves me. Anyway, I pay her for it.'

'Don't have a row, girls,' said Harry cheerfully. 'Here are the others.'

Toby, Edward's brother, came through the door with Alison, the vicar's pretty daughter, there to make up the numbers. He was impressive in his dark coat and white silk scarf. He had his own version of Edward's features – deep-set eyes, a square chin – but he was taller, and there was a wilder look about him; he looked the outdoor man he was, dedicated to his farm, with any spare time spent shooting, or out on one of his horses. Polly was fond of him, though she found him rather alarming. But he'd taught the girls to ride; he'd helped her out that awful night when Jessica had a fit and Edward was away and she couldn't reach the doctor. There'd been other times, too. Sometimes she felt she could really talk to him – then the distance would set in again.

They went into the parlour – the big drawing-room had been taken over by the Followers – for a glass of champagne, and on into the dining-room. The Followers, mercifully, didn't seem to like eating in there. Over the delicious meal – cucumber soup, smoked duck, summer pudding – Polly felt her spirits lift as they hadn't for months. Edward, pouring out an excellent hock for them all, had shaken off his gloom and the particularly annoying expression of concern he'd worn for some time whenever he looked at Polly. He chatted with Toby, teased Ruth and Muffy; by the end of the meal even Jessica was laughing, and when the three cars set off for The Gunnocks, they were all in high spirits.

Just as well, for the newly refurbished house demanded a major reaction. Within the rectangular walled courtyard the symmetrical front was brilliantly lit against the dark sky; huge torches flamed on either side of the double-leafed front door, held back by liveried footmen. 'How grand!' breathed Muffy. Polly remembered a rather unfortunate drawing-room wing which had been added in the 1950's, destroying the perfect balance of the design – this had been rebuilt and matched by a similar structure to the west, where huge glass windows reached to the floor. Here the earlier arrivals could be seen, the black and white of the men, the bright colours of the women's dresses.

In the hall, among great banks of flowers, they were greeted by the ball committee; local aristocracy, some money, a minor royal. Polly had been on it for a couple of years, but had found that the Byzantine machinations of her fellow members as they established their pecking order were too much for her.

They passed through to the new conservatory, Harry explaining the while the changes the owner had made to the house. 'He's had the floor sprung for dancing in here, though they've covered over the terrace as well tonight – there are two bands. Come on through, I'll show you the drawing-room. That's the dining-room in there.'

'And what does he use the other wing for?' Edward asked.

'Pictures – his own collection. They're quite something, and so is the security in there.'

'He's American, isn't he?'

'Not a bit of it, he's as British as they come, but he spent some time in the States and made his money there. Look, here are the murals.'

This high room, apart from the fireplace and cornice, was entirely modern; round the walls swirled great bands of metallic colour – flame, green, midnight blue.

'I'm not sure I like it – what a strange man he must be,' Polly said thoughtfully. 'Married?'

'Here and there, I think, but not now.' Harry grinned. 'He'll need a little wife, he's thinking of standing for parliament! I'll introduce you to him later.' He gave her one of his sweet smiles. 'Now, Polly, I hear distant music and it sounds like a golden oldie – all I want is the excuse to hold you really tight.'

Harry was a deceptively good dancer, and Polly enjoyed flirting with him; they set off cheerfully for the conservatory, stopping for a moment at the big table where the others were sitting. Soon most of them had left it – Muffy and Francie, after a few disgusted contortions, took the twins to the terrace where the music was newer and louder; Edward was dancing with Alison, Toby with Jessica. Kind Ruth was sitting with Robert, who, she knew from her friend's rather strained smile, must be telling her about his new car.

'It's just like the old days,' she sighed to Harry.

'Except, of course, it wasn't like this at all!'

'I know, I know,' she murmured, but the magical atmosphere took her back to the remembered world of her youth, and to the parties where she'd shone in borrowed finery. Perhaps it was the contrast with the recent dismal months – her worries about Ruth, the Followers like a sticky tide invading her two houses, the changes in Edward.

But when she danced with Edward himself, a few minutes later, he held her tightly, pressed his cheek against her hair. How good he always felt; apart from anything else, he was exactly the right height for her. He drew back a little as they chatted about the house, the dance, the people.

'Toby seems to be getting on with Alison.'

'Mmm,' she murmured. Why did she always feel a stab of jealousy when other women managed to talk so easily to Toby, and she couldn't?

'I wish he'd marry,' said Edward, who had a genuine fondness for his brother, 'but I'm afraid he never will. He could be a genuine old fashioned bachelor, they do exist – do you remember Uncle Gilbert?' How could Polly ever forget him, with his beautifully kept ancient Bentley, the fearful pipe he'd smoked all over the house? They laughed together.

'I do love you, Polly.' It was a long time since he'd said that.

'Oh, Edward, so do I!' More than ever, in fact – perhaps the recent distance between them had sharpened her appetite for him. 'Things are going to be all right, aren't they?'

She'd spoken without thinking – she knew he hated that kind of question. He was looking at her seriously. 'Of course they are; I know we'll all settle down at Cottenham. You do love that house, don't you?' He smiled down at her indulgently.

I prefer it without the Followers, she wanted to say, but, 'Yes, I can't wait to see how the rose beds do this summer,' seemed safer. Then: 'Talking of summer, Edward darling, you know we didn't get away in the autumn? Why don't we take a break now – we could spend a few weeks in France.'

'I'd love that,' Edward answered with real warmth in his voice, 'I really would love to spend some time at the château. We'll plan it. I should get in touch with Georgette, anyway, to check that things are in order there.' Georgette lived in the cottage at the gates of the château and, with her son, Hector, looked after it for them.

The dancers were dispersing and moving towards the dining-room where the buffet supper was laid out. Polly, still glowing, went back with Edward to their table to wait until the crush was over. Muffy was sitting there with a twin. 'Dad, a flunkey was looking for you.'

Sure enough, one of the exotically dressed attendants came up to Edward and handed him a message. Edward read it, frowning slightly. 'Polly, I'm sorry, I'm going to have to go – Jim's just arrived at Cottenham and he needs to see me urgently.'

'You mean you've got to go now?'

'Yes.'

Polly couldn't believe it. 'Edward, you can't just walk out on us in the middle of a party. Can't you ring him?'

'If he says it's urgent, he'll mean it. Will you apologise to the others for me, Polly?'

'No, I will not!' It burst out of her. 'Edward, you can't bloody well do this. Why should you be at his beck and call? You're behaving as if he's in charge of you.'

'Don't shout, Polly, people are looking.'

Indeed they were. Heads at the nearby tables were turning. Muffy for once had decided to keep her mouth shut; she whispered to her partner, who came hurrying back in a moment with Harry and Ruth, both carrying plates of cold salmon, rare beef and delicious salad.

Polly didn't care who stared; she felt wild with rage. She could have physically attacked Edward; at the same time she felt a dream-like incapacity for movement. He started to walk towards the door — she evaded Ruth's outstretched hand and managed to walk quite slowly after him. Halfway across the hall, he stopped for his coat. She caught him up.

'But you just said you loved me.' It wasn't something she had planned to say; it just emerged out of somewhere deep inside her.

His calm eyes looked at her. 'Polly, it's a question of priorities.'

'Can you just stop calling me Polly every second?' she shouted. 'You even sound like that frightful man!' There, she'd really done it now. 'Sometime soon you're going to have to choose between these people and me,' she said as she caught at his arm. He shook her off without a word, and she suddenly saw their scene with an outsider's eye — as ridiculous as real life always was. It would work better in an opera. She must say that to Edward; he would understand exactly what she meant. But Edward was already gone.

She couldn't go back to the others; they would be kind to her, and she couldn't bear that. She sat down on one of the long sofas in the empty hall; she felt unembarrassed by the presence of the two pantomime footmen, presumably they were used to scenes. She really wanted to be alone — in a minute she'd look for somewhere more private, there'd be a library or something; she knew there was a black-clad attendant installed in the lav, so that was no good. As she looked down she noticed a large unidentifiable mark across the front of her skirt — she must have brushed her new dress against something as she pursued Edward from the room. This was the last straw. She started to cry.

But, oh no, someone was coming towards her — a tallish, rather solid dark man with heavy eyelids and what remained of some dark curly hair. Beautiful clothes, Polly noticed dispassionately through her tears, and rather her type.

He sat down beside her. What a cheek.

'Are you all right? Can I help you?'

Polly took the handkerchief away from her face. She wasn't up to telling him what she would like him to do. 'I just want to be by myself for a while.'

'Why don't you let me take you through into the gallery? No one will be there.'

'But it will be locked.'

'Yes, I have the key. This is my house.' He paused. 'Polly, don't you remember me? Mark Jansen, Piers' friend. I can't have changed that much. And you don't look a day older, Polly; as beautiful as ever.'

In the gallery, Polly collapsed on a rather more comfortable sofa under an early Sidney Nolan. Astonishment had dried her tears for a moment, but now they were flowing freely, the product of mingled rage, misery and sheer embarrassment. Whatever were she and Mark going to say to each other when she did stop crying?

'I think you need a dry handkerchief,' he said as he gave her one, 'then a glass of champagne and some food. I'm going to arrange that. I'll be back.'

'Thank you,' she said – she suddenly did feel very hungry. 'Oh, and could you let my family know I'm all right?' She set about repairing the damage the tears had done to her face.

Half an hour later, they were still on the sofa. Polly had demolished a large plateful of lobster, and Mark had summoned up more champagne. His attention and the drink had banished Polly's tears – and some of her inhibitions. She had told Mark the pattern of her life – more or less – since she last saw him; he had told her about going to America and making lots of money in an esoteric branch of the electronics industry, and about his first ventures into the world of art. Piers was clearly next on the list as a topic. Mark spoke first. He must have read her thoughts.

'Polly, I suppose you still see Piers?'

'Not for ages now, though I keep in touch with Felicity. My

elder daughter, Jessica, is his child, you know.' Polly felt herself blushing – luckily the lights were low.

'I saw her – she looks just like you. So she'd be, what – nineteen?'

'Yes.' Polly nearly added, 'What a good memory you have!' but decided against it. 'And do you see Piers?' she asked in a bright, conversational tone.

'No,' said Mark, 'I haven't for a long time now.' He paused. 'I tried to ring you, you know, when things got so difficult between you and Piers, but I left it too late and you'd gone. Perhaps it was best we didn't speak.' He hesitated again. 'Polly, I just wanted to explain what it was between Piers and me, though I know it mightn't have helped. You see, for me, at least, it wasn't . . . It was just a . . .' He looked away briefly then smiled back at her. 'But it's probably too late for all this now, isn't it?'

Polly thought for a moment. Then she said: 'I'd like you to tell me sometime, maybe, but not now. It's all so long ago, after all.' And there were so many problems in the foreground, she didn't really want to add the memory of other miseries.

'That's good,' said Mark, 'because it means that at least I shall see you again.'

Polly looked at him in some surprise – she had found him extremely easy to talk to, and was by now rather taken with his unusual looks – could it be the effect of champagne and of the sheer smell of money, she wondered? He seemed to be suggesting that he rather fancied her. So had he stopped preferring boys? Harry had mentioned a wife, hadn't he? It was all too confusing. She picked at the mark on her skirt. 'Of course we'll see each other – after all, we're practically neighbours. And you must meet my husband.'

'Yes,' said Mark. 'Wasn't he here earlier? Could I ask why he left?'

'You could,' said Polly rather haughtily; but her misery overcame her again and she buried her face in Mark's handkerchief. Predictably, he put his arm round her; how funny, she thought, to be literally crying on someone's shoulder at my age.

She felt him turn, rather abruptly, and looked up to see Edward in front of her. A little behind him stood Jim Drogue, with Jessica beside him.

'Jessica told us you were in here,' Edward said. 'I came back because I was worried about you.'

'Good evening, Polly,' said Drogue. 'Edward, it looks to me as if your wife is being well taken care of.'

CHAPTER 8

Polly was woken at ten o'clock the next morning by the crash of car doors and raucous shouting; she staggered to the window to see the twins wedge Francie into the back seat of their old TR3 and take off down the drive. She staggered back to bed. She felt incredibly tired; possibly tired enough to stay in bed for ever . . . If only she could remember exactly what had happened last night after Edward turned up with Drogue. Perhaps she had been too drunk to take it all in? Polly yawned. At least champagne didn't give her a headache; it just made her feel incredibly tired . . .

The second time, Polly was woken by the sound of someone tuning a guitar in the room next door; the chords were joined by a voice she recognised as Adrian's admittedly excellent baritone:

'Morning has broken like the first morning . . .'

It was by now early afternoon; plainly, after their visit to Wembley, the Followers were reborn all over again. Polly thumped on the wall. The music ceased, only to start up again, self-consciously *sotto voce*, after a brief whispered conference.

Polly flung herself back on the pillows – and realised that the events of the previous night were now perfectly clear in her memory.

Somehow Mark had manoeuvred Edward and Drogue out of the gallery and back into the hall; she wouldn't forget the freezing look he had given the footman who had admitted them. She had followed with Jessica, who had led Drogue towards the conservatory, where the guests were still dancing; it was then well after two o'clock. Mark had stopped to talk to Edward; she herself, frozen with nerves and with the cold, for the hall was draughty after the controlled warmth of the gallery, had felt her coat put round her shoulders – Toby – and had then seen the two men part. At that point, she thought Harry and Ruth must have joined her, for the next thing she remembered was the drive home. Edward was not with them. Harry had obviously decided not to comment on his absence and was full of chat about the party – but Ruth had lain silently against her seat, looking iller and iller with every mile that passed, so that soon concern for her friend had overridden all Polly's other anxieties.

'Ruth, you're white as a sheet!' she said as soon as they were inside the house. 'You're exhausted. Let me help you up to bed.'

'Poll, you are kind,' said Harry. 'I'll just have a spot of whisky before I come on up.'

Arm in arm, the two of them had rustled to Ruth's bedroom, and once inside with the door shut, Polly had asked: 'Ruth, are you ill?' Stupid question.

'I've been having some tests – I'm going in to get the results tomorrow. I'll be all right.' Clearly she didn't want to talk about it further. She turned to Polly and said effortfully: 'But how about you? I actually caught a glimpse of Jim Drogue – at least, I suppose it was him – when he came back with Edward. When you left for such a long time, I thought you two must have made it up. What happened? Can you tell me?'

'I will, but not now – we're both too tired. We'll talk in the morning. Shall I unzip you? Here's your nightdress.'

Out of her dress, she had seen that Ruth was painfully thin . . .

Remembering, Polly sat up sharply in bed and reached for the phone. Ruth and Harry would have gone home – she must give Ruth a ring.

But though she tried several times, there was no reply. She began to wonder whether there was something wrong with their own phone – it wasn't unusual. Since there was no sign of Edward, she could only assume he'd gone to London and though she didn't quite like to ring him, surely he would have tried to ring her. And she rather expected a call from Mark. She'd have to get up and try the line in the stable flat, or ask Sandra to do it for her.

There was a knock at the door.

'Oh Sandra, it's you! I was just going to come and find you to try the telephone in the flat. I've got an awful feeling that the line's out of order again. I wanted to ring London.'

'I'm afraid I've come about something else, Mrs Lonsdale. I wanted to have a word with you.'

Polly had heard this formula too often not to feel a sinking of the heart – the words people had wanted to have with her, from Muffy's various headmistresses through a succession of absconding staff, had never been to her advantage. She'd have to dress, anyway.

'I'll be down in a minute, Sandra. I shall be in the dining-room.'

Sandra seemed to be lingering, but Polly didn't feel she could face anything without putting her clothes on. 'I'm sure you're busy, Sandra: I'll come on down.' Sandra departed.

The sooner she got this over with, the better, whatever it was; Polly decided to skip her usual bath. Her days as a model had made her a quick dresser; twenty minutes later, immaculate, with the unnaturally pink cheeks and bright eyes of a hangover, she was downstairs.

The dining-room was already occupied. To her great surprise, Sandra, at the head of the table, wasn't alone; Meg, in the over-familiar pink cardigan, Meredith, looking more like a goat than usual, Judy and Bethany were all sitting round the table.

Dozens of little vignettes from the past months came into Polly's head: Sandra beaming at Jim Drogue; Sandra arranging flowers in 'our prayer room'; Sandra wanting to go to Wembley; Sandra cooler towards her, less willing than before. Not for the first time in her life, Polly cursed her inability to take in the obvious – with her eye for detail, she often missed the broader outline. But then Sandra had, after all, been her admiring aide-de-camp for sixteen years; as far as Polly was concerned, she was a mildly ludicrous figure who had made their comfortable lives possible, who could be relied on to support Polly in everything she did. Of course she had taken her for granted; now, evidently, the worm had turned and Sandra was in a position to take revenge for all Polly's offhand moments and casual kindness.

She had learned her lesson well, and sat at the head of the table commandingly. But it was Meg who spoke first, her spectacles gleaming.

'We have been praying for the right path, and it seemed best that we should speak with you as sisters; of course our brother Followers have shared this decision with us. Would you like a cup of tea? You don't look well.'

'No.' Nor would you look that well if you'd drunk the amount of champagne I did last night, thought Polly. She felt a wild desire to fling herself the length of the polished table and strangle Meg with the thong which supported the cross on her chest. 'So what do you want to speak to me about? I'm not used to being summoned to little meetings in my own house.'

A look passed between the women.

'Mrs Lonsdale – Polly – we feel that you need guidance.'

'Does my husband know that you planned to sit in his dining-room passing judgement on his wife? If that's what you're thinking of doing?'

Meg and Sandra smiled at each other.

'No, Polly, but we work and pray as a team,' Meg said. 'We know that he and Jim wouldn't wish you to continue in error. Isn't that right?' she appealed to the sisterhood. There was the low murmur of assent which more usually interspersed their prayer sessions.

'When you say error, what on earth do you mean?' asked Polly, genuinely interested to see what they would come up with.

Sandra spoke next: 'We don't just mean the incidents of last night, Mrs Lonsdale . . .'

Incidents? The row with Edward, her head on Mark's shoulder? How would they have known about either, as they'd been praising the Lord at Wembley? Had Edward told them? Jessica? It had to be Drogue, of course.

'. . . I'm afraid word of your behaviour has reached us, but we can overlook a momentary backsliding or two. No, Mrs Lonsdale, they were only the culmination of the life you have been leading; a life of sin and deception.'

'How dare you speak to me like that!'

Judy's brown curls were bobbing in her earnestness. 'Mrs

Lonsdale – Polly – there is still time to take another way. Jesus loves you – we know He does – He wants you to come back to Him. We know you have hardened your heart to His message, but He is there, waiting – waiting for you to be reborn . . . We want you to pray with us, to hear the message of His love . . .'

There was something hypnotic in the words. All she could see of their faces was the gleaming spectacles – why had she been so foolish as to sit with her own face in the light? What did they know?

'You must leave this house. I shall speak to my husband,' she said. Somehow the words didn't convince even herself. Once again, the women exchanged glances.

'Edward will be praying for you, as we are,' said Meg. 'He has finally come, through God's grace, to a full understanding of his error. He wanted – no, he knew it was God's will for him – to take some time apart, to drink in the Word, to pray. We have all persuaded him not to be harsh, to take pity on a sinner. But,' she added in a more businesslike tone, 'he realises that we, the committee of the Followers, have great works in hand. We have to have a base. We shall be staying here. Edward left this letter for you.' Bethany brought it round to Polly – sure enough it was Edward's minuscule writing, superscribed 'By Hand'. 'Now, Polly, Sandra has found a passage of Scripture which we could read together. Let us help you. We are only the humble channels of God's grace, which He longs to pour out on you.'

Polly got to her feet – at that moment the door opened and Muffy's face peered round it. She gave the women a glance of open hostility and beckoned to her mother. Polly found herself out in the hall, clutching the letter.

'Mum, look, a whole armful of orchids for you!' No message – it had to be Mark.

'They're lovely, but what am I to do with them? Dad's left a letter for me. Muffy, be a dear and make me a cup of tea. I may need to sit down to read it.'

'Come in the kitchen by the Aga, your teeth are chattering. Where is Dad?'

'London, I think. Muffy, I don't quite know what's happening.

Where's Jessica? What's she up to? She didn't exactly help things along last night.'

'I'm sure she's around somewhere. I know you had a good old row, but I thought you'd sorted it out.' Muffy peered anxiously at her mother. With the resilience of the young, she showed no trace of the activities of the night before. Polly repressed the desire to ask her how she'd got back, where she'd been. She knew she would be putting off the moment when she had to open the letter.

Dear Polly,
It may seem strange to you that I am writing – it certainly seems strange to me. Among other things, we've very rarely written, have we? Postcards and telephone calls, always, when I was away.

I felt it would be best to get down on paper my feelings and plans for the future. You will realise, after last night, that the situation between us is radically changed. First, and as so often, you seemed to be unaware of any needs other than your own. Secondly, when I did return to you with Jim, whose presence I felt would be helpful in view of the hysterical condition in which I had left you, I found you in the arms of our host. I'm afraid the explanation he gave me did not, on later reflection, convince me. You can imagine my reaction, let alone Jim's feelings, on witnessing this scene.

I know you feel I am overly influenced by Jim. Rather, I am following, under his guidance (and of course the guidance of the Lord) the way that I should have taken many years ago. I cannot blame you, Polly, for my backsliding; yet I cannot help but feel that our first meeting was the work of Satan, followed as it has been by a life of sin.

Jim has been my support and help in the decisions which I have had to reach, and which cause me no little sorrow. You and I must part, at least until you can abandon your cynical attitude to Jim's work and to the Followers – and until God's grace, for which we are all praying, leads you to the new life that is still possible for you if you will only open your heart to Jesus.

Obviously we have to address ourselves to practical matters –

I don't want to make things difficult for you. As you know, Connaught Square is more or less taken over by the Organisational Executive of the Followers. Sandra's flat would be available to you for a short while; her duties will be divided between London and Cottenham, where she will be acting as Divisional Group Director – in this way her administrative abilities, which you have for so long overlooked, will be fully enabled.

Very shortly we shall start adapting Cottenham as a base for training both new and established Followers, so space will become extremely limited there and I shall have to ask you to leave. I regret not having shared this with you earlier, but your attitude was so hostile that I feared your response would be negative.

I shall of course make such provision for you as I can, given that an increasingly large part of my funds and income will be absorbed by the Followers. I would suggest that you find modest rented accommodation as soon as possible.

As for the girls, I am of course delighted that Jessica too has been touched by God's grace.

Muffy is still a minor, and I shall expect her to make her home with me. Away from your influence, we feel she may have a better chance of altering her rather frivolous ways and, with us, seeking the true path.

With God's blessing, yours in Christ,
Edward.

Polly sat for a minute, her head bent, with the letter in her hand. At first she had had to believe it was some kind of joke or trick; the handwriting was undoubtedly Edward's, but the curious mixture of business language and religious jargon could almost convince her that the whole thing had been dictated by Drogue. There was too much of Edward in the letter, however, for her to hold onto that as even the most forlorn hope; and something told her, some instinct for survival, that this was not the time for hope, that she had to reserve all her powers for action.

A great sadness stole over her as she looked again at the first paragraph; she did indeed remember their times apart, the calls in the small hours of the night from the other side of the world (efficient Edward could never master the time difference), the scribbled postcards that so often arrived after his return. And she remembered their times together; at Cottenham, the trips to Paris and Rome, that holiday in Africa, the evenings dressing companionably to go out, or dining at home and watching television through to the late-night movie.

Was it all gone, never to return? Even if this was a passing phase of Edward's, hadn't it already scarred their relationship irrevocably? Was the glimpse she had had last night of the old Edward a sign that he would come back to her, or that false brightness you see just before the sun sets?

Her tears had all been shed the night before, as if she'd already been certain of the outcome of that evening. If only she hadn't let herself go quite so dramatically! Yet she knew, with the dull certainty of experience, that her embrace with Mark was neither here nor there; Edward's feeling for her had already been doomed.

She felt something hot against her hand, and looked up to see Muffy thrusting a mug of tea at her; they'd put all the good china away, out of the reach of the Followers. The child's blazing eyes were fixed on her. For an instant, hatred for her rose inside Polly, all the hatred her numbed feelings couldn't accord Edward. He wanted Muffy, but he didn't want her! Muffy and Jessica were to be included in their cosy little club – she, Polly, was to be left outside. She would show Muffy this lunatic letter, to punish her.

Muffy had recoiled before the look in her mother's eyes – now she put out a hand to her. 'Mum, what is it? Why is Dad writing?'

'I'm sorry I was like that, Muffy. I frightened you, didn't I? I've got to tell you – Dad's leaving me; at least, he wants me to leave. It's all right, you're to stay with him.'

'But why, Mum, why? Is it to do with last night?'

'Yes, a bit, but it's mainly because he doesn't feel I'm in sympathy with his Christians. I'm afraid Jim Drogue's been getting at him.'

'He'll change his mind!'

'Muffy, it'll be too late. We can't go on like this, anyway. It might be best if I did go away for a bit.'

'But where?' asked Muffy.

Polly looked away. 'He's suggesting I rent somewhere. I'll think of something.'

There was a small silence, then: 'I'm coming with you!'

'Muffy, it won't be anything very grand. I shan't be able to afford much.' She couldn't believe she was actually having to say this.

'Of course you will! Dad'll have to make you a proper allowance – after all, you're married. He'd have to give you a fortune if he divorced you! But it's not as bad as that, is it? Everything's so awful at the moment!'

'No, Muffy, we won't get divorced. We can't, you see – we never got married.'

CHAPTER 9

Why on earth had she told her, and now of all moments? Did she have some awful desire to punish her? Muffy went even paler than usual, then bright red.

'Mum, you naughty girl!' she exclaimed. 'You mean I'm a genuine, old-fashioned bastard?'

'Well, I suppose so,' said Polly doubtfully. A terrific grin spread over Muffy's thin face.

'If only I'd known! I thought I was born in boring old holy wedlock, like everyone else. So that's why you were a bit shifty about showing me wedding photos, saying they hadn't come out and so on. But why didn't you and Dad get married? It was always just as if you had.'

'I just never got around to getting a divorce from Piers; then you know your grandmother was so starchy about divorced women, she would have hated Edward to have married one, and it would have been bound to get back to her. Technically, I suppose I'm still married to Piers.'

'You mean, technically I'm the daughter of that pansy?'

'Muffy, please. Well, yes, you are. None of it seemed to matter much.' At least the turn their talk had taken had temporarily put an end to the frightful pain Polly felt – why did people always say it was in their hearts when it fact it was in the stomach? For a few minutes she had felt almost cheerful; then it hit her again.

'Mum, we've got to think of what we're going to do,' said Muffy urgently. 'For a start, I'm sure you can get Dad back.'

'I don't know. Oh Muffy, I must.' And Cottenham, she thought. Abstractedly, she handed Muffy the letter.

'I see what you mean,' said Muffy, when she'd read it, 'but it's worth a try. I'm going to go to London to talk to Dad.' She paused. 'Oh, Mum, d'you really think Jess is in it too? I know she's been a bit weird lately, but I never thought . . .' Then a small grin spread over her face. 'I suppose all that guilty bit is because you're living in sin?'

In spite of herself, Polly laughed – surprising Bethany, whose droopy head appeared round the door at that moment. She withdrew hastily.

'Muffy, for heaven's sake don't go; you can stay here with Jessica. I must find Jess and talk to her. I can't believe she's become part of this thing. Where is she? I haven't seen her all morning.'

At least the search for Jessica gave her a sense of purpose. But Jess wasn't in her own room, or the kitchen, or the sitting-room. Perhaps she had gone out for a walk.

The Followers must still be closeted in the dining-room – they weren't around, apart from Bethany, who was forcing the younger of her wailing children into a stuffy-looking multi-coloured anorak on the front steps.

'Have you seen Jessica?' Polly asked her; Bethany, wrestling with a hand that had got stuck down a sleeve lining, didn't hear, or didn't want to answer. Polly noticed a great bare scar on the gravel – the twins, she supposed, and sighed. Drogue's BMW was missing, and Edward's more familiar Mercedes.

As Polly rounded the house, she almost ran into Robert. They both spoke together: 'Have you seen Jessica?' Polly added: 'I thought she would be with you.'

'No.' With that curly hair growing so low on his forehead, Robert really did look like a not-too-intelligent bull. 'She got up early this morning – she was rustling around in the room, then she went out.' In his anxiety, Robert neglected to keep up the pretence that he and Jessica didn't sleep together at Cottenham. They circled the house again, and walked past the pretty lead statue of

Psyche down towards the wall at the bottom of the garden, Rosie gambolling after them. Polly noticed that the lilies in the herbaceous border would need staking, the huge clump of white daises should have been divided up; I'll have to speak to Mr Gandon when he next comes, she thought – then the reality of her new existence struck her. She wouldn't be here to tend the flowers, or anything else. Cottenham would no longer be hers.

'I can't think about it now.' She hadn't realised she'd spoken aloud until she saw Robert looking at her curiously. They were now at the bounds of the garden – no sign of Jess. Because of their shared quest, his evident distress, she felt more drawn to him than she ever had before.

'Blast the girl,' he said. 'I need to be off. Couldn't we ask some of those frightful people if they know where she is? That Drogue chap?'

'Good idea.' Even as Polly spoke, the picture of Jessica and Drogue in the gallery the night before came into her mind. She turned to Robert as an awful suspicion began to form.

'You don't think . . . do you think she could have gone somewhere with him?'

'With who?' Her fellow feeling for Robert diminished – he was so very slow on the uptake. 'Oh, with Drogue. Why the hell should she? You don't think she's run off with him?' He laughed heartily at the idea; he was far too vain even to contemplate Jessica's defection with another man when she'd got him.

'No, not exactly, but apparently she's got quite interested in all this Christian thing. You know how, er, impressionable she is.' When he'd talked of marriage, they'd told Robert something of Jessica's problems – by tacit agreement, these had since been glossed over. Well, it was hardly the sort of thing you'd discuss endlessly with a prospective bridegroom, was it? There was certainly no point in getting Robert rattled now.

'Tell you what,' he said, grabbing her arm as they walked quickly back to the house, 'as you can't ring, I'll check out that lot to see if they know anything, then I'll get down to London and see what's going on.'

They pushed through the back door and bumped into Sandra,

carrying a pile of leaflets through to the drawing-room. In her anxiety, Polly had almost forgotten their earlier meeting. 'Sandra, do you know where Jessica is?' she asked her, before Sandra's frosty, newly self-important expression reminded her.

'She left before lunch.'

'With Edward?'

'With Mr Drogue. Now, if you'll excuse me, I need to arrange our prayer-room. We're expecting our first group of trainees tomorrow morning, by the way – if you need any help while you sort your things, I'm sure Judy or Bethany would be delighted to look after you. I'm afraid I can't make it my responsibility any more.' The scorn in her voice was unmistakable.

'What the hell ...' Robert took a step forward, but Polly restrained him. As Sandra moved on with her leaflets, he turned angrily away, pulling his keys from his pocket.

'I'm going after them!'

'Oh, Robert – but I suppose you'd better. I'd come, but I ought to sort things out here.' Edward might still come back.

A few minutes later she watched him drive round the corner of the house and away and when he had gone she just stood in the hall, leaning against the wall. Here, above the panelling, the old plaster was painted a lovely faded salmon-pink. She ran her fingers down it, remembering how she'd planned it to go with the grey of the flagstone floor, and how pleased Edward had been with the result. A huge copper bowl of pink paeonies stood on the oak gate-legged table. All this was her doing. Cottenham was hers by right, she wasn't going to lose it.

A door opened and she heard the scraping of chairs on the wood floor of the dining-room, a buzz of talk and the clatter as the Followers moved into the hall. There seemed to be more of them there already. Suddenly she felt a wave of hostility emanating from the old house. Edward wouldn't come. For now, there was nothing to be done here; she knew she must go, but where? Ruth, of course; Ruth and Harry would take her in. But what about Muffy?

Muffy, when consulted, insisted that she was going to London to talk to Edward, and to see if Jessica was there with Drogue. Since Muffy had demonstrated at the age of a few hours old that if she made up her mind about something, nothing would change it, Polly agreed to this, though with some misgivings. She could drop her at the station on her way to Ruth's.

Urged on by Muffy, Polly summoned up some extraordinary reserve of energy. She packed a small suitcase. She found that the phone was now mysteriously functional again, and briefly rang Harry; he sounded surprised, but of course she would be welcome. She decided against trying to ring Edward. Halfway down the drive, she remembered that she had neglected to tell anyone in the house that she was going; what the hell, they could work it out for themselves.

At the station she said goodbye to Muffy – she saw tears in her eyes now, and they clung to each other for a long moment, parting only to see a huge pearly Rolls, carrying Mark Jansen away from the little arcaded brick buildings. He nodded gravely as he passed.

Polly nodded back, rather distantly; then, too late, remembered those gorgeous vulgar flowers – she could at least have smiled her thanks. Perhaps she should have pinned one on her coat? Did anyone do that any more? And what would happen to the orchids – another hideous pottery vase in the makeshift chapel, she supposed. The thoughts which kept flitting through her head at least distracted her from the dreadful pain of her loss, which she knew would hit her again. She wished she had begged Muffy not to go – as she drove off, she badly wanted her company, and the thought of that brave little figure setting out on her mission had touched her deeply. Then suppose Edward and Drogue – and he had to be behind that extraordinary letter – persuaded Muffy to stay, to join the Followers?

All this and more was going through Polly's head as she bumped down the track on the final stretch to Ruth's. She remembered, belatedly, the way her friend had looked last evening – it seemed like a year ago. Perhaps there'd be a chance now to find out how she really was – after she had told Ruth about her problems. Ruth was the one person who would understand; she would say straight out what chance she thought there was of Edward coming back to her. His letter, already crumpled, was in Polly's hand as she slammed the car door; she would show it to Ruth straightaway.

Harry came to the door; as he led her in Polly immediately noticed the unmistakable tang of ancient soot, and glimpsed through the sitting-room door the gaping hole where the fireplace had once been, and beside it two bags of cement and Harry's coffin-sized tool box. He took her into the kitchen, and she saw with gratitude the half-empty bottle of whisky on the table. How thoughtful they were: Ruth must have known she would be in a do and had got it ready for her, though she felt dubious about having any more drink, especially at four-thirty in the afternoon.

'Harry, I think I'd prefer just a cup of tea. Where's Ruth?'

'Hospital.'

'Oh no, the test results! I'd forgotten that she was going in today. Poor Ruth. Oh Harry, I've been having such a time! Edward has run off – well, he hasn't, but he's told me I've got to leave, which is worse really, I suppose. He's written me this dotty letter, I know that frightful man Drogue dictated it to him. I was going to show it to Ruth, but could you look at it for me and tell me what you think I ought to do!'

Harry was still silently filling the kettle at the sink; when he turned, she finally noticed how worn he looked, years older. And he hadn't even heard the full story of her troubles yet. She knew how fond of her he was, but she'd no idea that her problems would have this effect on him.

'Harry, you are sweet to mind so much! I know that you and Ruth will be able to think of something!' Even in her despair, waves of relief swept over her; they were her friends, her rescuers, they'd look after her and get Edward back for her. Edward liked and respected Ruth, he'd listen to her. She was still in her coat – she took it off and laid it down rather carefully, for here too the surfaces were covered in plaster dust, while she waited for Harry to finish fiddling with the teapot. Finally he spoke.

'It's cancer.'

'What do you mean?' What was he talking about? What could

cancer have to do with it? Unless, she thought wildly, Harry had knowledge she did not. That could be the answer; Edward had a brain tumour, hence his recent behaviour. All this flashed through her mind while the real sense of his words came home to her.

'You mean Ruth has got cancer? Is that why she was looking like that? How bad is it?'

'They're still not quite sure, but it doesn't look very hopeful. They would have operated right away when they took her in, but she's too weak. Oh, Polly.' He put his head down on his arms on the table; as Polly rose slowly to fetch the tea, she saw him stretch for the whisky bottle. 'Polly, I'm so sorry about you and Edward. Tell me.'

Polly opened her mouth to do just that – then stopped. 'Harry, it doesn't matter, I'm sure it's nothing, he'll be back. To think of me bothering you when Ruth might . . .' She couldn't say the word; the very thought was too terrible, let alone her shame that, locked in her own problems, she hadn't realised that something was so badly wrong with her friend. But why did it have to happen now, just when she needed them? She tried to stifle the selfish thought.

'When did you know about this?'

'No time – it seemed more of a possibility a couple of weeks ago, and she's been having these pains and losing weight for some time. She never told a soul, you know how she gets on with things, so it's gone really far – and if only I'd thought of it in time, I could have got her to a doctor. I was busy with The Gunnocks and I never noticed.' He put his head on his arms again, and when he looked up she saw that he was weeping. What a lot of tears there have been today, Polly thought wearily. She moved the whisky bottle a little further away, and pushed his cup of tea at him.

'Drink this. Go on. Have you eaten?'

'No, not since I took her in.'

'I'll make us something,' Polly said; she had never felt less like cooking. Now that she doubly needed the comfort she had come for, it seemed that she was to become the comforter. She put her hand on Harry's head in an age-old gesture; he caught her wrist and kissed it. 'Darling Polly, it's so lovely to see you. You're the one person in the world who could understand how I feel.'

'Does Dave know yet?'

'No, I'll have to ring him. To tell the truth, I'm rather putting it off. You'll help me, Polly, won't you?'

As they ate, Polly felt better; she realised that she had been very hungry, and the practical details of looking after someone else had a distracting novelty. But when they had taken their coffee into the rather comfortless sitting-room she realised that she felt, for once, uncertain with Harry – did he want to talk about Ruth? She found it hard to phrase her own questions, for they all had a note of solemnity that was foreign to her usual banter with him; finally she did manage to ask – was Ruth in pain – what were her chances?

'It's not too bad – they're starting her on serious drugs,' was the first uncomforting response – and apparently they had said, under pressure, that she did have a chance of recovery.

Survival. Polly sat silent, her head bent, for how could she respond? While she dreaded facing the changes in her friend, she longed to see her. Surely she would be able to resist the temptation to pour out her own troubles, which already seemed rather remote – she'd actually forgotten about Edward for an hour. She wanted to thank Ruth for everything, to seek her blessing. If only she could be magically transported to her bedside! A frightful weariness made the darkening evening outside, the unknown journey to the hospital, take on almost mythical proportions – like some test which a hero of long ago would have to undertake. But she put the possibility to Harry.

He shook his head. 'She's drugged, she'll be asleep, they'll never let us in. We'll go first thing tomorrow.' He looked at her. 'But Polly, you must keep it light – she doesn't know yet how bad it is.' He saw her crestfallen face. 'I'm sorry, darling.'

How thoughtful he was for her feelings, dear Harry. Polly took his hand and asked more questions, got him to tell her the story of

Ruth's symptoms and tests from first to last; and as he talked, Harry gradually relaxed. He told her about the hospital, which had the usual farcical overtones of such institutions; when they arrived, Ruth, who had walked normally through the door, had been clamped into a wheelchair and not allowed to move thereafter. For now she was in a room with a pathetic teenager whose husband sat silently beside her, and a gigantic Greek woman whose entire family perched on her bed long after visiting hours, plying her with food. Another occupant, the wife of a policeman, had an astonishing trousseau of swansdown-trimmed satin negligées. She was rather above the other patients, and obviously pitied Ruth her worn cotton nightie and towelling dressing-gown.

'But Harry . . .' Polly guiltily remembered her own brief sojourns in the London Clinic; she was never quite sure how Ruth and Harry stood financially, up and down probably, with the fortunes of Harry's business. 'Is it the very best for Ruth, shouldn't she be somewhere private?' She would pay for it, if Harry would let her! Then she remembered her own now rather doubtful financial situation.

'She never would – anyway, it's a marvellous hospital. They do have a few private beds, but the nurses hate them – apparently you can ring the bell for a week and nobody comes.'

After a time he started to ask Polly about the Followers and what they believed in. She could feel that, now, distraction was just what he needed, and launched into a full account.

'They believe every word of the Bible. Well, not quite everything, not the Creation story I don't think, they aren't truly fundamental. They're very strong on Jesus, poor God is quite in the background – and as for the Virgin Mary! Well! You know we had that lovely statue of her in wood, Edward bought it for me in Barcelona because she had such a sweet face? That was shoved in a cupboard when they came to the house. I asked why, and Adrian – that's the group leader person – looked very chilly and said they could respect the mother of the Lord without idolatry. They pray a lot.'

'What sort of prayers?'

'Nothing set, except the Our Father, and they change the words of that – they seem to make them up, it's quite a gift, except I suppose you'd get good at it if you practised. They do it out loud, and raise their arms in the air, like children reaching up to Mum – it's rather touching, in a way. And they pray for things the whole time – actual things, very specific, like a microwave for the flat, or an architect. A Christian architect, would you believe it! Doesn't it seem rather impertinent to you, telling God exactly what you want? My granny used to tell me to simply pray for God's will to be done. They're very keen on love of course, but again they're a bit choosy – they didn't love me one bit, I'm afraid.'

Harry smiled warmly at her. 'But why not, Polly?'

'I hate to say it, Harry, but I think it was a social thing, rather. It's not that they don't like money and big houses, they seem to take them quite for granted – God's grace, they call it – but they didn't like my clothes, they didn't like anything that was different from them. I tried to join in once or twice, eating with them and so on, but the food wasn't up to much, a terrible lot of chewing; we had to hold hands at the beginning, for a great long grace, and you know I can't bear touching people I don't know. They do an awful lot of hugging, and none of the women wear bras – you're pressed right up against their bosoms.'

Harry laughed, then stopped abruptly. 'Edward will never stand it for long, mark my words; it doesn't sound at all his thing.'

'Well, he didn't have to put up with quite so much of that – they work at two levels. Jim Drogue and the ones in London aren't a bit like that – it's all Armani suits and BMWs, off to the States every five minutes. I couldn't stand much of that either, mind you – but anyway, they don't seem to let women into that side of it. They really do regard them as inferior – and believe you me, you don't have to look far through the Bible to find a few texts to support that one. Harry, I just don't know what will happen about Edward. And now Ruth, poor Ruth. Oh, Harry, I am so sorry.'

But Harry clearly couldn't bear to start talking about Ruth again. He began on the ball, and their intriguing host.

'He's an amazing man, there's no doubt about it. He built up his gallery from nothing. He's got a real eye for painting, and courage; a lot of the things he bought he got well before the artists were anything like as famous as they are now, and he's always prepared to back new painters. He was marvellous over the house, too; he had really clear ideas, but he let the builders get on without interfering. I like him.' He smiled at her. 'So he made a pass at you, did he, pretty Polly?'

'I suppose you could call it that.' The events of last night now seemed as remote as Mark and Piers on Hampstead Heath.

'Well, I'm not surprised, you're as lovely as ever. I'm so glad you're here, Polly.' Harry drew her down beside him on the sofa and put his arm companionably round her. Polly could just hear the distant sound of the river. How quiet it was, how wonderfully quiet after the thumps and twangings of the Christians: 'We like to keep lively for Jesus!' one of them had said.

Her head dropped onto Harry's shoulder; he turned to kiss her on the lips. As his other arm stretched round her, she reached up, her hands round the back of his head, and pulled him more closely to her. A swatch of fabric patterns, sent to Ruth for promotion in her magazine, fell unregarded to the floor. They kissed and kissed, hands desperate on each other, stopping only to laugh at their total discomfort on the sofa. Polly felt as if she was flying – a strange peace and the sensation of the years slipping away as her memories took her briefly back to her last embrace with Harry, in a London flat somewhere, a good eighteen years ago. How could she have forgotten the dear, comforting familiarity of his body? But he was pulling away from her; she lifted her face to his, only to see him smiling down at her with loving eyes. He smoothed back her hair and said, as he might have to a child:

'Bed, I think.'

Polly followed him up the stairs; by mutual agreement they turned into the spare room. There, in the cold, Polly took off her clothes even faster than she had put them on. Harry put out the light and joined her under the icy sheets. He started to stroke her all over, gently, as though to see if she was real. Polly, impatient, pulled him to her, and they made love as if they had been waiting for this moment all their lives.

CHAPTER 10

They were woken by the shrill sound of the telephone in the next room; cursing, Harry staggered naked out of bed to answer it. He called out to Polly: 'It's Muffy, she's in a phone box, can we pick her up from the station – oh hell, it's cut off. I'll go, Polly, while you dress.'

'Thank God she's O.K. I'll come too. Did she sound all right?'

'Couldn't tell – you know how it is with those things.'

They snatched a cup of tea downstairs, and got into Polly's car. She felt surprisingly natural with him.

'Polly, that was lovely. I know I should feel bad about it, but I can't. And I know how hard it's going to be not to do it again.'

Polly looked at him, surprised – of course they were going to do it again. Somehow, when they had been making love, she hadn't thought of the future. She wouldn't think of it now, she couldn't. Harry, Muffy, Ruth, Edward – each of them seemed to be occupying a separate part of her. Harry wouldn't leave her now – though there was Ruth . . . All she knew was that she couldn't give him up now, not for a little while, not after last night. She smiled at him, and heard his sharply indrawn breath as she put her hand on his thigh.

'You're a wicked woman, Polly!'

'Not really; if I was a genuine witch, I'd put a real spell on you. Harry, I know it sounds a bit odd, but after we've collected Muffy, could we go and see Ruth?'

Harry's head turned to look at her so quickly that he nearly drove the car into a giant vehicle, bristling with important-looking spikes, which was trundling down the road towards them. Over its noise, and the roars of abuse from the driver, Polly shouted: 'Don't worry, of course I'm not going to tell her all! I just awfully want to see her.'

Harry kept his eyes ahead. 'All right. I'm sorry, Polly, I thought for a moment . . . but of course you wouldn't. Yes, you go – but do remember, she doesn't know how ill she is.'

What a lot of lies I'm going to have to tell, Polly thought. And now they were at the station, in front of whose peeling facade and gaudy travel posters stood bedraggled Muffy, wearing a heavily-studded leather jacket over what appeared to be a green lace evening dress. She waved languidly and walked to the car.

'Have you had breakfast?' asked Harry.

'No, I'm starving, I caught the first train.'

'Let's find somewhere to eat, then.'

This was never the easiest thing to do in a smallish market town at eight o'clock in the morning; having rejected the station buffet, they finally struck it lucky in the market square itself, where a café had opened up for the stall-holders.

'How did it go?' Polly asked Muffy, looking about her with some interest; she'd never been in a place like this before. Then, nervously: 'How was Edward?'

'Bad. It started well; he was pleased to see me, and we talked for a bit. He said that if I really wanted to I could stay with you after all, Mum, so that's something, isn't it? But then I asked why he'd written you that letter and he said . . . he said . . .' Muffy's head dropped over her sausage and chips '. . . he said he meant every word of it, and he can't see you again unless you see the error of your ways. So I asked him "what ways?" I didn't know whether I was supposed to let on that I knew you aren't married to him.' Harry dropped his slice of toast, his face mirroring the amazement of the other breakfasters, who had been listening in to Muffy's rather carrying narrative. 'Oh, Mum, I am sorry – I forgot that nobody else knows.'

'Ruth always knew, but I asked her not to breathe it to a soul, that's why she didn't tell you, Harry. And I don't think it matters much who knows now. Go on, Muffy.'

'So I went on at him for a bit; I said if he'd married you – well, taken you on the way you are, which I think is fine, more or less – and if it was him that had changed, then he could hardly expect you to change as well! But he wouldn't listen – he carried on about new paths, and the way of the Lord. Then Jim Drogue came in, and started trying to charm me; he could see that the Lord was at work in me, and so on. He even had a go at bribery – he sort of said that I could join their training school in the States, even though I'm young for it. Then I'd be part of the jet-set Christians, flying all over the place to extend their mission.' Muffy waggled her head vigorously from side to side. 'No way was I signing on.'

'So then what happened?' asked Polly. There was a pause.

'They got in Jess.'

Harry laughed. 'It would sound like the Inquisition, if Jess wasn't really rather a dear!' But Muffy's face was solemn with the awfulness of the news she bore.

'Mum, *she* really *is* thinking of going off somewhere – perhaps it's to America too – with Drogue. She's obviously been a bit in love with him ever since that first evening when they walked in the square. She gazes at him with those great big beddy-byes eyes' – Polly hastily removed her own from Harry – 'I think she'd jump off a cliff if he told her to.'

'Did she say anything?'

'That was the amazing thing, she talked and talked. She just went on and on at me to sign up and find the path of peace or whatever. I was flabbergasted, and didn't know what to say. So in the end I just said I was tired and I'd go to bed.'

The whole café was silent by now; even the girl who'd brought them their breakfast had suspended her lethargic wiping at the counter in front of her. Let them all listen, thought Polly, it really doesn't matter. She felt almost detachedly fascinated by Muffy's story; her main desire at the moment was, after Muffy was sorted out, to get back to bed herself, with Harry, and away from it all.

'Then I went up to my room. But after about an hour I thought I couldn't stick it – but when I tried to get out, I found they'd locked the door!'

'Well, that's not right!' came a voice from across the café.

'Too right it isn't, to treat a kiddie like that!'

Muffy continued, now well aware of her audience: 'So I got out of the window, down onto the extension, then the back wall and round the house, like I always do. Then I got the train here.'

'Excuse me, Muffy, but what do you mean, "like you always do"? Do you mean you've climbed out of the house before?' Polly's voice began to rise to the standard pitch of the outraged mother; the patrons of the café, sensing that the dialogue had taken a rather more familiar turn, began to drift away.

'Of course I have, Mum, I thought you knew.'

'But it's miles up, you could have killed yourself! How long have you been doing it for?'

'I don't know, since I was about twelve, I suppose.'

'Twelve!' Polly turned to Harry, but one look told her that his mind was somewhere else – in fact he had hardly spoken since they had sat down. 'Harry?'

He seemed to come back from a long way away. 'We'd better be getting on, if you want to see Ruth.'

'But aren't you coming too?'

'No, I'll go in later – they don't like more than one person out of visiting hours, anyway.'

'But . . . Muffy, I think that secondhand clothes stall over there is opening up – just your kind of thing. I'll be out in a minute.' Muffy looked from one to the other of them, and tactfully went.

Polly turned to Harry and took his hand. 'Harry, do come with me.'

'I couldn't face Ruth if I did. Give her this for me, will you.' He gave her a parcel. 'Polly, last night was wonderful – ' the girl behind the counter was transfixed again, and he lowered his voice ' – but that has to be the end of it.'

'I could come back home with you – we could be there together till Ruth gets better!' Or doesn't get better, the horrible, disloyal thought went through her head.

'It would have been lovely – but we can't. Anyway, Polly, how about Muffy – she could hardly be there with us. Let's go outside – that girl's clearly got hearing like a bat, let alone the old girls in the corner.'

Outside, it had started to drizzle – the market traders, cursing, were heaving tarpaulins over the stalls, and the granite cobbles were greasy with the rain. Droplets beaded Polly's fur. Muffy could be seen on the far side of the square, picking rather listlessly at a counter of bric-à-brac. They drew under the shelter of an awning which proclaimed 'Finnie's Fancy Goods'; the shop window featured a good selection of china cottages, baskets of pot-pourri and flowered vases.

'So you're leaving me?' It didn't seem quite the right question, but Polly couldn't think of a better way of putting it.

'Polly, I'm not leaving you – of course we'll see each other again, and be dear friends. Last night was just one magic time, we both know it – I've got Ruth to think about, you've got Muffy. Go and see Ruth – I know you won't breathe a word – then sort things out with Edward. We'll be in touch.'

He's dumping me, thought Polly, stupefied; he just doesn't want to be bothered. That's the second man who's dropped me in one week. Last night meant nothing, it was a comfort to him, nothing more. It was no use making a scene; what he had said was all too true. She managed a strained smile which seemed to make her whole face ache.

'How will you get back?'

'Oh, I'll get a cab or a bus or something. Don't you worry about me.' He kissed her lightly on the cheek, and turned down one of the side-roads.

Muffy was back. 'Mum! Look at these beads! For a moment I thought they were jade – it's not as good as that, but they're lovely Victorian glass ones, and only three pounds. Aren't I clever?' Polly held her close for a moment, then started to make her way to the car.

The hospital was a huge, many-windowed concrete block on the outskirts of Ipswich. As soon as they passed through the automatic doors into the over-heated, brightly lit foyer, Polly's heart sank into her leather boots. 'Wait for me here,' she said to Muffy in her most casual voice. 'I shan't be long.'

At the end of a maze of antiseptic corridors, she found Ruth's room. Six beds; her eyes took in the fat Greek woman Harry had mentioned, and that must be the satin-clad policeman's wife. And there by the window, oh God, was Ruth. So pale and thin, poor Ruth. No, she couldn't bear it, she would have to leave and come back another time when she felt stronger.

Ruth had seen her. Smiling painfully, she instinctively sat forward to greet her friend, then fell back on the pillow with a little cry of pain.

'Oh, my poor Ruth – shall I call a nurse?' Polly, who had been standing irresolutely by the door, moved quickly past the other beds towards her.

'Please, yes – the drugs are wearing off. There's a bell . . .' Polly rang it.

'What do they give you for the pain?'

It was shocking to see how hard it was for Ruth to talk. 'I'm pretty sure it's nothing but good old-fashioned morphine, though of course they give it a fancy name!' She smiled weakly. 'Polly darling, you are good to come – I can't talk much, it hurts so.'

'I know – I'll only stay a moment – but I did so want to see you.'

'How are things with you and Edward?' Ruth whispered.

'Oh, we'll get sorted out, don't you worry,' Polly replied – the first of the lies she was in for.

'I'm so glad. And have you seen Harry?'

'Yes. He gave me this for you. He'll come in later.' Polly handed over the package.

Ruth's hand moved faintly on the sheet. 'Open it for me, there's a dear.'

'I will, but I'll just go and get a nurse first – they don't half take their time round here.'

Polly went down a corridor hung with gaily coloured abstracts and past mysterious rooms full of chrome equipment, to the desk where two nurses were bent over their paperwork. Her furs and her best commanding manner sent one scurrying to the drugs room. Back with Ruth, she opened the untidy parcel.

'What on earth? Oh, there's a letter – I'll open it for you.'

Ruth read aloud: 'Dear Ruth – There WAS a little cupboard behind the fireplace, and this is what I found there. Isn't it lovely? Please get well, my darling, I miss you so much. All my love, always, Harry.'

Polly felt a terrible pang at these so clearly heartfelt words of love. Whatever had happened last night had obviously been, for Harry, quite separate from his feelings for Ruth, which ran as deep as his very being. For all the admiration she aroused, nobody would ever feel like that for her. Polly brushed away the self-pity and took the contents of the parcel from Ruth. It was a flat, buckled leather shoe – eighteenth century? – in a size which would now fit a child.

'It's a talisman to make you well, Ruth,' she said firmly. Nothing more should ever come between them. She put her arms gently round her as the nurse came in with a sinister looking syringe.

Muffy was waiting on a leatherette sofa by the lift leafing through an ancient copy of *Woman's Own.*

'How is she? Did you give her my love?'

'Forgot to, Muffy – I'm sorry.'

'Oh, Mum.' She got up. 'I know it's cancer – but where, exactly?'

'You won't believe this, Muffy, but I still don't know. Somehow I got past the point of asking, then I felt as if it was too late. She's very bad.'

They trailed out to the parked car.

'Now what, Mum? We can't really go back to Cottenham – shall we risk London?'

'I couldn't face it, Muffy – we've got to find somewhere to stay.'

There were, of course, dozens of people to whom Polly could have turned. She and Edward were part of a wide circle of friends and acquaintances, with whom they dined, holidayed and went to the theatre. All of these were the owners of at least one capacious house, and most would have been delighted to put up one, if not two, guests for a finite period of time – and, should it be necessary, to provide further help with accommodation; a friend of a friend would have a flat vacated by a grown child, a couple would offer space for a house-sitter while they took off for six months.

Polly could picture it all, and the faint smiles that would accompany the kindest of offers; she could hear the ringing of the telephones that would bear the news of her downfall around London and Suffolk. Everyone loved to do a kindness, especially one that was so cheaply bought, so near home – excellent to give money to dying Romanian babies, but how much better to have the object of your charity so clearly, so gratefully in view. And even the most generous of friends would get something of a *frisson* out of the fact that beautiful Polly had finally got her come uppance.

No, she could no more bear the pitying smiles than she had been able to in the early days when she had broken up with Piers . . .

Of course . . .

'I'm not sure what we'll do, Muffy,' she said, almost cheerfully. 'But before we do anything else, I think we'll go and see Felicity.'

With a brief diversion off the M25 for a late pub lunch at Chevening, they made it into West Sussex by teatime; as they turned off the main Brighton road the lanes became more and more familiar, and when they finally entered the Broadbridges' drive with its high banks of fern, to emerge in the unkempt courtyard in front of the main farmhouse, Polly thought she had never been more relieved to arrive anywhere. As always, she tried the ancient bellpull at the front door, and as always, no one answered; she and Muffy went round to the back.

There, in the huge, filthy old kitchen, sitting in a wicker chair by the Aga, they found Felicity. She was shrouded in shawls and scarves: the stick she'd recently taken to using to help her get about stood upright by her chair, and one of her many cats was seated on the hem of her voluminous skirt. Since Tristram's death three years ago, she had become even more eccentrically herself; Polly thought she looked eerily like a witch.

'Well, well,' Felicity said, her eyes bright with interest. 'Polly.

And Muffy too. How very nice. Let me organise some tea, and then you can tell me why you're here.'

Tea was set out, and later cleared away, by Piers' sister Alice and a beautiful young boy Polly had never seen before, called Darren; they drank Earl Grey, and Muffy stuffed herself full of carrot cake. Polly felt warmed through by the gentle heat of the Aga, strangely comforted by the familiar eccentricity of her surroundings. When they had finished, Felicity produced a tin of small cigars from under her drapes and lit up and Polly began her story. There was something compelling about the stare of Felicity's black eyes, the beringed hand stroking the cat on her knee – resigned to the cigar ash that dropped onto his back. When at last Polly had finished, there was a long pause.

'So,' Felicity said at last, 'you've got rid of Edward. Quite right too, he was always a bit of a bore.' And as Polly opened her mouth to deny this heresy: 'You can't say he wasn't, and don't start telling everyone he left you, that's quite the wrong approach.'

For the first time in her life, Polly felt the courage to confront her mother-in-law. 'I came here for some advice, not to be laughed at!'

Felicity did laugh then, a surprisingly youthful sound. 'Glad to see you full of spirit – especially under the circumstances. You've lost Edward, you've lost Jessica, you've lost Cottenham!'

Jessica. For some reason, the deep anxiety she felt about Jess, which she hadn't had the courage to face till now, seemed suddenly to surface in Polly and clamour for attention. Poor, simple Jessica, deluded by these people. 'I'm so worried about Jessica,' she said. 'I simply hadn't noticed how involved she'd got with the Followers. And that awful Drogue man. I don't think she'll come to any real harm, but ... I don't even know if she's up to looking after herself!'

'I shouldn't worry,' Felicity said surprisingly. 'She's a big girl now. And a new experience like this might shake her out of her problems – have you ever thought they might be to do with people mollycoddling her all the time?' She stared shrewdly at Polly. 'Now don't get huffy. Let's think about what you're going to do.'

'There's lots of things we could do, aren't there, Mum,' put in Muffy, stroking away at a huge tortoiseshell and a small grey kitten that were occupying her knee. 'I could stay with someone and you could go and live at the Savoy!'

'Muffy, I do have some cash,' Polly said slowly, 'but I think we'll have to be quite careful until things are sorted out with Dad. And after that, I'm afraid we may find ourselves living in pretty reduced circumstances.'

There was an exasperated sound from the wicker chair. Felicity pushed her familiar from her knee and, using her stick to theatrical effect, walked over to the Aga where she stood as if in front of an altar. 'Giving in, are you?' she demanded.

'Well – ' said Polly.

Felicity gave her the benefit of another of her penetrating black stares. 'You can sort these people out, can't you, a tough, resourceful woman like you?' Polly felt her jaw begin to drop. 'Oh yes, don't imagine I've ever been deceived by that beautiful, fragile-looking exterior and that charming, helpless manner. I knew there was character there the first time Piers brought you to see me in that ridiculous little pink skirt.' She smiled. 'You need a strategy, Polly. A plan of campaign.'

'But what sort of plan?' said Polly. 'The Followers is a big organisation, it's powerful. I wouldn't know where to begin.'

'Join them,' said Felicity sharply. 'Find out about them. Find out who their leader is, and what his game is. Find out what makes them tick. Then you can get rid of them.' She lit another cigar. 'You can stay here till you find a place of your own, and meanwhile – ' she drew in a lungful of aromatic smoke ' – I'll give you some lessons in survival.'

CHAPTER 11

To her surprise, Polly found a flat for herself and Muffy within three weeks. It was in a pretty old house in Camden Town; the couple who owned it had been happy to let it, it had been on their hands for months after their marriage. Muffy was delighted with it; if she leant far enough out of the window she swore she could even see the park. She had loved staying with Felicity, the interesting people who inhabited the farm and outbuildings, and their interesting activities, had been a constant source of fascination – but she was equally taken with her first sight of Camden Town, with its casual bustle and transient population. Polly was less ambivalent about escaping from Felicity's rather overpowering presence; she defiantly sent details of her new address to Connaught Square, to Cottenham, and to close friends.

She and Muffy took possession on a chilly day in late April. Polly pushed open the front door, stiff from lack of use. There were some letters among the junk mail inside. Her heart lifted as she saw Edward's tiny writing. She opened the envelope with shaking hands – inside was a cheque for £1,000, accompanied by the briefest of notes: 'I am shortly going to Russia, on Followers' business.' Russia! Oh, Edward. A letter from his solicitor came next; 'matters were in hand'. What matters? A straggly card from Ruth – she'd seen her last week. Nothing, nothing from Jessica.

Finally, a letter that turned out to be from Mark Jansen. It was almost indecipherable. Occasional words were clear: 'disappeared . . . I shall be . . . week'. She took it through to the window of the big back room, where Muffy was unpacking.

'You need glasses, Mum. Do you want me to have a go?'

'I certainly don't,' Polly replied huffily, then: 'Have a look, I can't make it out.' Muffy took the letter.

'It's easy. It's from that man who owns The Gunnocks. He said he's away until the end of this week, then he's going to ring and hopes he can take you out to dinner. Hey, you really did make a hit there, didn't you, Mum? I wish I had a rich admirer.' Muffy sounded wistful, and as Polly looked at her she suddenly realised what Muffy had been through in the last few weeks – she'd lost her home, her father, her sister.

'Muffy, are you sure you wouldn't be better off with Dad, when he comes back? I'm sure he still wants you, you know. And it's going to be pretty miserable here – he's sent some money, but I'm not sure where the next lot will come from.' As a last resort, she could sell her jewelry; she made a vow to keep the brown diamond ring, her favourite.

Muffy thought for a minute. 'I do love Dad, and I miss him awfully. But it's all different now he's tied up with Jim Drogue, and they've taken Jess. I might go back to him in the end, but I'd like to stay with you for now,' she said. She looked so young and vulnerable that Polly had to turn away to hide her own face. She would have given the world, at that moment, to make her happy.

'Muffy, I want you to have this big room for your own. And look, it's only six o'clock but I'm starving. Let's get a Chinese takeaway; I saw a place down the road, I haven't had one for years. We can leave the rest of the sorting out till later.'

It was the best she could do.

While they were unpacking the foil dishes from their brown carrier bag, the phone rang. 'Hello, is that Mrs Lonsdale? This is Miss Hugh-Richards speaking. I've been trying to get you but I was told you're at a new address. I know Cordelia has been with us only a short time, and that you may be unfamiliar with our dates, but I must remind you that the Easter holidays ended two weeks ago, and your daughter has still not returned.'

Horrors! Polly had completely forgotten about school. 'Yes, Muffy – I mean Cordelia – is with me. I do apologise; she could come to you tomorrow, or perhaps the day after. I'm afraid we're a bit disorganised at the moment.' Totally disorganised, in fact. But her grovelling had softened Miss Hugh-Richards' heart; she was obviously experienced enough to spot all the signs of yet another family break-up.

'Well, we shall look forward to seeing her, though it is a little unfortunate that she should have missed so much of the summer term.' Understanding Miss Hugh-Richards might be, but she wasn't going to lose the opportunity for censure.

Polly, making faces at the phone, had been too taken up to notice Muffy's wild gesticulations from across the room. When she had put the receiver down she said: 'Did you get that, Muffy? I forgot to send you back to school. Sandra would have reminded me in the old days. Why are you waving your arms about?'

'I'm not going back, Mum.'

'But you must! You can't leave school now – you've got your GCSEs this term!'

'I don't care. Anyway, all my uniform's stuck in Connaught Square. I'm going to get a job. Let's eat that stuff, there's nothing nastier than cold Chinese.'

Polly, who longed to keep her but knew she couldn't, was intrigued in spite of herself. Muffy had always been irritatingly vague when the ritual questions about a possible career came up. And whatever could a totally unqualified sixteen-year-old do? A dreadful vision of the pale girls she'd seen on her visits to Edward's factory came back to her. 'Muffy, if you're worried about the money, don't. When we run out, I'll find something to do.'

If it was hard to envisage Muffy working, it was ten times harder to see herself in a job. Muffy laughed, with unnecessary scorn, Polly thought. 'I know you were a big success in your time, Ma, but the models are all about my age now. I think you're unemployable. Maybe you could learn to trim hats, like poor Lily Bart in *The House of Mirth*.' Polly was notoriously unhandy.

'Thanks a lot – and didn't she kill herself in the end? Muffy, you'll have to go, you know. I'll be brave and ring Sandra; we'll get round there tomorrow and fetch your things, and mine. I'm sorry darling, but school it is.'

'*I* shall kill *myself*!' Grumbling, Muffy retired to the back room to throw the clothes she had with her out of their bag.

Polly sat on in the darkening sitting-room – beyond the curtainless windows the lights were lit, the clatter of shutters as the shops shut gave way to the sounds of the evening. She was comforted by the obvious presence of people around. She started to remember the evenings in Connaught Square – just around this time she and Edward would have been sitting down to dinner, with or without company . . . Deliberately she brought her thoughts back to the present.

How odd it was that Felicity, who she thought had always rather despised her, had turned out to have such a high opinion of her resourcefulness. She wasn't at all sure that Felicity was right, but certainly her advice seemed to be the best course to follow. 'Put Jessica out of your mind for the moment,' she'd said, 'and concentrate on clarifying your own position. Once you've done that, you can think up a few plans for those Followers or whatever they call themselves.'

She'd taken the first step – talked to a solicitor Toby had recommended. Poor Toby, he had been so distressed by her situation; he had offered her financial support, which of course she'd refused, and made strenuous efforts to get in touch with Edward, without success. As he said, being Edward's brother he was in a rather ambiguous position – but at least he could find her a good solicitor who could explain to her her legal position.

But the solicitor had said that, without the full facts, and in the absence of Edward – Polly had invited him to the meeting but there'd been no reply – the situation wasn't very clear. However, if Cottenham had been leased to the Followers for ten years, and the leases were foolproof, that was it. 'Unless they voluntarily relinquish it – in which case it would be returned to its previous ownership,' he'd added casually. The position was much the same with Connaught Square. On her rights, he was less than positive. 'I'm certain your partner will provide for your under-age daughter – but the position of abandoned cohabitees is, to say the least of it, unpromising.' For a moment Polly had wondered who he was talking about – the realisation that it was herself was the final spur to action.

It was a long time, forever in fact, since Polly had planned anything more elaborate than a dinner party, though that could take some doing. So how on earth could she think up a campaign against an organisation as powerful as The Followers seemed to be? Most of the members she'd met were a joke, and Jim Drogue didn't scare her either; but though as individuals they might not be intimidating, together – as a large, well-organised body of people with contacts abroad and friends in high places – they were a force to be reckoned with. Perhaps the most frightening thing about them was the power of their message; that they could take over someone like Edward so completely.

Oh, Edward. With all her heart she longed for him, but not the Edward of that frightful letter, or indeed of those previous months. She wanted him as he'd been, as they'd been. Surely this change in him wasn't for good? Shouldn't she just wait for him, forget about the Followers? But it was only through them that she could get Jessica back . . .

Her brain raced – she took a deep breath. Felicity had suggested that, as well as everything else, she might want to get even with the Followers – with disloyal Sandra, with smug Meg, with Adrian, with Drogue, with the lot of them for invading her house, stealing her daughter, her husband, her life. It was true! And she'd get back Cottenham while she was at it!

But how? 'If you can't beat them, join them,' Felicity had said. But how to join them? She would have to fake conversion, a complete change of heart. Could she make that convincing, did she have the nerve, the sheer histrionic skill? And how and where could she stage her dramatic entry into the Followers' fold? Details were important; the whole thing must be properly judged.

Polly wondered if she could call on anyone to help her, give her at least moral support. Not Harry – poor Harry, he had trouble enough of his own. Toby? But she didn't think Toby was really the man for this kind of enterprise. Mark Jansen?

Polly thought about Mark; he was clearly only too willing to embark on a relationship of some kind – though exactly what kind, it was hard to be sure. Was she keen to investigate the possibilities? Might he help her with her plan? He certainly had lots of money, and no doubt the power that went with it. Polly thought wistfully of the luxury of The Gunnocks, of those sumptuous orchids – the lavish little dinners and even more lavish little presents she might be denying herself if she turned her back on him. But the fact was that, the more she thought about it, the more it seemed to her that she must do what she had to do alone.

Suddenly, she felt immensely tired. She couldn't think any more now. And Felicity had counselled patience and careful planning – there was no rush. She'd mull it over – and meanwhile deal with the practical matter of getting her and Muffy's things out of Connaught Square.

She looked at her watch and saw that it was past ten o'clock; the Followers were probably tucked up in their virtuous beds by now. Never mind, it would do them good to have their routine disturbed.

As she picked up the phone she found that her mouth was dry with hope and fear – was Edward still there? Suppose he answered? Perhaps she might even get Jessica. Instead, she heard Sandra's voice. After she had put her request, there was a long silence.

'I'll make arrangements for you to be let in,' Sandra said at last. 'In fact, I'd better be there to supervise the removal of your personal possessions.' The servile note had gone from her voice; these were the brisk tones of the mistress of the house. Polly left the phone, seething.

They went round early, Polly fortified by a stiff brandy – she had no idea, still, whether Edward would be there, or Jessica, but she took the precaution of putting her appearance in order. Sandra let them in. With one corner of her mind Polly took in her rather flustered look, but she was too preoccupied with her own emotions to pay Sandra much attention.

She'd known it would be hard, and now that she was here she could hardly bear to cross what had been her own threshold until so recently. A thousand memories met her as she walked into the hall. Unthinking, she had read of people dying of grief – now she felt that she might. Luckily the grief was tempered by so much good, healthy hatred as she looked at Sandra's smug face, that she felt new resources of strength springing up within her.

'We'll start at the top, I think,' Polly said, in a voice of such authority that Sandra quailed, and meekly mounted the stairs.

In the bedroom she was overcome all over again with agonising nostalgia; the room was exactly as she had last left it, even down to a jacket carelessly thrown down on a chair. She managed to indicate to Sandra which drawers of clothes she wanted – fortunately the woman knew her wardrobe inside out. The furniture here meant little to her, but she snatched the peacock feathers out of the jar. 'I'll take these now.'

'As you like,' said Sandra.

She asked Sandra to pack all Muffy's things – Heaven alone knew where they'd put them, but she felt it was important. They went downstairs – here everything had changed. In the drawing-room the red-robed cardinals had been banished from the walls and replaced with photographs of groups and individuals; she recognised Jim Drogue among them, then Edward. Her sofa, her tables, were gone, and in their place stood ranks of gilt-and-velvet chairs. There was something else. Suddenly she realised that every bookshelf was empty.

'Where are the books?'

Sandra smiled faintly. 'We found that a number of titles were unsuitable in a Christian setting. As Bethany used to be a librarian, we asked her to sort and dispose of them.'

'And where's my Bristol glass?'

'You needn't worry, Mr Lonsdale will be communicating with you,' Sandra replied.

Polly turned without a word into the dining-room – more gilt chairs were gathered round her own table, lengthened by all its leaves. She couldn't bear to look further. As she moved into the hall, the door bell rang. 'Oh, that'll be the . . . the van,' Sandra said as she hurried to the front door.

Muffy had disappeared into the garden. Polly, free of Sandra, decided she'd take one last look upstairs. Obviously, neither Edward nor Jessica was here. She felt painfully sad.

She walked into Edward's study; perhaps she'd find some clue to his new self. His desk, always tidy, held only some small posters advertising a Followers' rally, a set of proofs – apparently an article for *The Christian Businessman* – and a pile of unopened letters. There were footsteps on the stair, but no one came in. She leant her head miserably against the window-pane. Outside, the view was unchanged; in front of the house was a good-sized transit van with 'Fletchers' Clearances' painted on the side. Clearances? As she puzzled, two young men came down the steps, carrying the rocking-horse from the old nursery.

Polly was through the hall and out into the road in a flash. 'What are you doing with that rocking-horse?'

'We've been told to clear that top room out,' said the taller of the two young men in a strangulated upper-class accent. The smaller one, who had tattoos and a striped, piratical-looking T-shirt, just stood and grinned. Neither of them looked much as if they were Christian clearance men.

'But it's mine!' Polly shouted.

A voice spoke from behind her – of course, it was Sandra. 'Excuse me, Mrs Lonsdale, everything in the house – apart from your personal goods – belongs to Mr Lonsdale and Mr Drogue. We need more space; Mr Drogue has asked me to make arrangements to extend the accommodation for our members. We are planning a new suite of guest-rooms – with bathrooms, of course – on the attic floor.'

Polly stared at her. 'Sandra, how could you? You know how the girls always loved that horse, and the toys.'

The taller young man, fingering his earring, was listening to the debate, torn between interest and the desire to get on with the job, get paid and get away. The small one had disappeared into the house, presumably to fetch more of the contents of the attic.

The smile remained on Sandra's face. 'There are different kinds of love, Mrs Lonsdale, and we all feel your daughters are ready for fuller, more creative relationships. We must put away childish things.'

So Sandra had been involved in spiriting Jessica away. She knew where she was! Polly threw caution to the winds. 'Where's Jessica? You know, don't you? Tell me!'

Sandra's eyes remained on hers, but they clouded over in just the way they always had when she'd been asked to do something she didn't want to. She wasn't going to tell, that was clear. But by now Polly was frantic.

'Well, you listen – if those boys don't stop, and leave that stuff alone,' she hissed, 'I shall scream so loudly that everyone will come out of their houses.' Memories of an earlier drama in the square gave her inspiration. 'And when they do, I shall show them those rows of chairs, and tell them you're setting up a business here. You'll have the residents' association after you in a second, let alone the council.' Polly realised she was still clutching the peacock feathers; in fact the locals would probably think she had gone mad, but it was worth a try.

'Oh, I'd have to ask Mr Drogue about that.' Now Sandra looked uneasy – she'd flushed with alarm and anger.

'You'll do as I say, you stupid woman, or you'll all be out of here!'

Both young men were now watching, with increasing exasperation, but as Polly turned to them she saw the expression on the face of the small, piratical one turn to delighted amusement – as Muffy came through the door, clutching a garden gnome.

'I'm not leaving poor Fred behind. They can get themselves a Christian gnome if they want one.'

'That chap was really nice, wasn't he?' Polly and Muffy were back in their flat, hardly able to move for the contents of the nursery.

'Yes – they were a bit fed up at not getting to sell all that stuff, they would have cleaned up, some of those old toys are really valuable – but fifty quid wasn't bad for a couple of hours' work, I told them. It was lucky you had the cash on you, Mum. They should be here in a minute with our clothes and things – it was much better us packing them ourselves. Doesn't the rocking-horse look just right there? Oh, and by the way,' Muffy opened her leather jacket, 'I got these.' She produced a grubby cloth bag.

'The snuffboxes! Muffy, they were in the safe – how on earth . . .?'

'I've known the combination for a million years, silly Mother. They're yours, aren't they, from Grandpa? We can sell them.'

'Muffy, you're wonderful!' Polly fished in her bag. 'Look, I brought something back, too.' She unrolled the poster she had taken from Edward's desk; it shouted in bold black script: 'CHRIST FOR THE WORLD – follow Christ with the Followers!' and gave the details of a rally to be held in a fortnight's time. 'Muffy, I'd like to go. I know I've had enough of the Followers to last me a lifetime, but there are still all sorts of things I don't know about them – like who's their real leader, for a start; it's not Jim Drogue. What about you coming with me? You and Francie could have the weekend off school.'

'Aha Mum, do I feel a plot coming on?' Muffy gave her mother an evil grin. 'Of course we'll come. Anything for a laugh!'

Muffy spent her last night in the flat in a nest of long-outgrown dolls and teddies. When Polly looked in on her, asleep, she was lying quite still on her back with a line of them down either side of the bed and a stuffed lion under her feet, like a crusader. Polly was tempted to change her mind and keep her – but the next morning, disconcertingly, Muffy packed her own things, donned the maroon blazer – how long ago it seemed, that day she'd first tried it on – and announced that she was ready to go.

CHAPTER 12

Polly felt a social anxiety she hadn't experienced in years as she entered the conference centre where 'Christ for the World' was being held. She'd insisted that Muffy and Francie sat elsewhere; grouped together, they would be far more conspicuous, but now she felt some regret as they moved into seats on the far side of the aisle. They'd dressed the part, Francie's sizable bottom stretching a grey tracksuit, Muffy unrecognisable in a patterned blouse and an old pleated linen skirt of her own.

'What a good little girl! Just what you've always wanted, Mum!' she'd said in front of the mirror.

Polly herself had refused to go to any great lengths; she'd simply tucked all her hair up into a scarf, toned down her make-up and put on a boring ribbed cotton jersey dress she'd never liked. But now she felt intensely noticeable, for the women in the auditorium divided sharply into two types. There were the standard Followers with their sensible haircuts, spectacles, neutral cardigans and baggy trousers; they came in all ages. Then there were a breed she hadn't spotted before – clones of Jim Drogue's Charlene, from what she'd heard of her; they wore self-consciously pretty printed dresses, or pastel suits with toning blouses, pussy-cat bows fluttering at the throat under careful make-up, all topped by elaborate hairdos in unlikely colours. Still, Polly could hardly be seen; she was seated well away from the stage, and there must be more than a thousand people streaming in. Among them were a few quite famous faces; Polly noticed a television presenter, and the beautiful, notorious daughter of a duke.

Among the last to arrive were the group from Cottenham; Polly recognised Meg, Adrian, Bethany – no sign of Sandra. Instinctively she buried herself in the handsomely-printed programme they'd all been given, unlikely though it was that they would look in her direction. She glanced over to see whether Francie and Muffy had noticed them; to her horror she could see that they were giggling together, and that Francie had taken off her tracksuit top to reveal acres of abundant white flesh and a minuscule halter top. She longed to signal to them to be quieter, but to attract their attention would only make both herself and them more noticeable, and she could already see heads turning in their direction. There was nothing to be done.

She distracted herself by looking around the huge hall, which she had once visited for some gathering after an international trade fair in which Edward had been involved. The Followers had certainly made a good job of it. Behind the rows of seats was a massive display of posters and piled books. The walls had been hung with banners silk-screened with Biblical texts, not all of which she recognised – had they made them up? The lighting was expertly arranged to highlight these, and a huge multi-coloured cross was projected onto the ceiling; not exactly subtle, but effective. On the wide podium a stately row of gilded chairs made a curved line, flanked at its far ends by the usual paraphernalia of an orchestra. Over it all a banner declared 'Jesus – the world is ours'.

The lights dimmed, and the voices hushed (Muffy's too, Polly hoped) as the orchestra and choir, white-clad, took their places. The doors closed firmly, and in the half-light Polly noticed dark-uniformed men, shirts buttoned to their necks, standing at regular intervals along the ends of the rows. Did they expect trouble?

The dim light, the soft music, were hypnotic – and then suddenly there was a blast from the trumpet, a magnified clash of music, and a figure centre-stage was exhorting them to Rejoice! The curtains at the back of the stage opened; the principal dignitaries filed in. And there was Sandra, herself unrecognisable in a smart pink suit, a cluster of flowers at the lapel, with newly auburn hair. Riveted, Polly almost failed to notice that Edward was beside her;

but as she saw him, a pain ran through her like a knife. He was back, but he hadn't got in touch with them. How could he do this? And what about Jess? Drogue was here, but where was she? Polly's resolve hardened as Jim Drogue took the centre of the stage, and the microphone.

'As most of you will know, our Leader is unfortunately unable to appear.' Damn, thought Polly. But perhaps Drogue would at least say who he was? 'However, he has sent a welcoming message to all of you tonight, to all of you who are willing to share our message and that of the Lord Jesus . . .'

For Polly, the rest of the evening passed in a haze; figures on the platform rose and spoke, their exhortations interspersed with songs from the choir, hymns in which the audience joined with an ever-growing frenzy of excitement. The guest speaker was a well-known MP who had been tipped as a likely Minister of Education in the next cabinet shake-up – almost sobbing, he spoke of the breakdown of morals among the young, about the duty of all Christians to bring Jesus into the schools – a new Children's Crusade, he called it. Polly's historical knowledge was a little vague, but she seemed to remember that the last one hadn't ended too well; didn't all the poor little things die on the way to the Holy Land? But the audience was rapt, and when Drogue finally called for those who truly wished to bring the Lord Jesus into their lives to make a visible commitment, there was a rush to the front of the hall.

Edward had disappeared. Polly longed to leave – would that make her too conspicuous? But she felt she should see it out, and a kind of fascination, let alone the presence of the daunting minders, held her there. The lights finally came up; she sidled out into the aisle to meet Muffy and Francie by the door, as they'd arranged.

Had she missed them? The chairs they'd sat in were empty, and she'd reached the door quite early. On the stage a queue of acolytes were still having their names and addresses taken by more men in uniform. There was a huge throng at the back of the hall, where Drogue and the MP were signing copies of their books; triumphant, pink-faced purchasers forced their way back through this crowd with their trophies. Was Muffy among them? But the book-buyers thinned away, and still there was no sign of the two girls.

They could simply have left without her, there was no reason why they couldn't find their own way home. But the uneasiness Polly had felt all evening was increasing. Could Muffy have voluntarily signed up? Impossible, particularly with Francie in tow. Could the Followers have abducted her? Not that unlikely – they'd taken Jessica, with or without consent, and the whole emphasis of the meeting had been on the salvation of the young. It might seem melodramatic, but she wouldn't put it past them. What a fool she'd been to sit apart from them, to let Muffy out of her sight, to bring her at all! Damn the girl. She had to find her, and quickly.

Giving up all pretence of keeping herself hidden, Polly turned to a pair of the guards who stood near the door; reassuringly they wore the uniform of a well-known security service, so at least she'd be spared their blessings.

'Excuse me, I'm looking for my daughter.' The man's brown eyes were watchful, but quite kindly. 'Have you seen her? She was wearing a . . .' Polly's voice trailed away; usually Muffy would be easy enough to spot, but her disguise was so effective, she would be truly lost among the young Followers.

'She's a kiddy, then?'

'No, she's sixteen, she's with a friend, but I was meant to meet her here and she's disappeared.'

'Well, a sixteen-year-old would be all right, wouldn't she? As all right as they ever are, I've got one myself. You want me to page her?' He raised his phone.

'No, oh no, please don't bother. I expect I'll find her.'

Polly turned back into the hall. By now the men in uniforms were beginning to disappear; other young men, in jeans and bright sweaters, were tidying the chairs, unplugging the wiring on the stage – one or two of them glanced at her.

As so often in a crisis – the day when Jessica had fallen out of a tree and fractured her leg, that time when the car had broken down at midnight in the middle of France – she was overcome by a kind of deathly lethargy; she wanted to close her eyes until the problem went away. But Muffy was missing. Perhaps the most sensible thing to do would be to go home and wait for her to turn up, as she most probably would. But suppose she didn't? Suppose she was still somewhere in the building?

Polly remembered from her previous visit that the main hall was surrounded by smaller meeting-rooms, and she turned into one of these. No sign of Muffy, though a huge chart boldly lettered in black fibre-pen indicated that the Followers had been there:

F	ELLOWSHIP
O	NE GOD
L	ORD
L	IFE
O	NLY BEGOTTEN SON
W	ORSHIP
E	TERNAL LIFE
R	ISEN CHRIST
S	AVIOUR

In a corner, some less reverent scribe had written 'Balls'.

She could hear the murmur of voices, safely remote. She walked through a lobby into the next deserted room; in the dimmer light, she could see the outlines of stacks of the crisp cardboard boxes which had contained the books on sale. There was no further door, and no Muffy. How absurd to think she would ever find her in this maze; how absurd to think she was here at all! There was a faint, spicy smell of expensive aftershave – she couldn't remember what it was called, she'd tried some, for fun, in Harrods.

As she paused, she heard a footfall behind her, and the door closed. Her worries for Muffy, her dream-like state, were replaced with a sharp, enveloping sense of fear. This empty, exit-less room was perfect territory for an attack – there was no one near enough to hear a scream for help. It was with actual relief that she recognised the by now quite familiar outline of Jim Drogue.

'Mrs Lonsdale – Polly.' He didn't seem very surprised to see her there.

'Where's Muffy?'

Even as she spoke, she realised that she could be giving away the fact that they had been spying. But Drogue's forehead wrinkled: 'Muffy?' he enquired gently. Of course, he never could remember her name. Now he was smiling at Polly as one might at the very young, or the mildly demented. 'Polly, we were so glad to see you here tonight'. So she'd been spotted; could it have been Edward? 'I have known that God would lead your footsteps to us. And I can see that you are already changing your ways.' He looked approvingly at her dreary dress, something of a contrast to the low-cut ball-gown in which he'd last seen her. 'It is Christ who is making these changes in you, Polly, the Lord Jesus Christ who is the master of us all. Don't you feel him calling you to him? "You who are fallen from grace, salvation beckons." Oh Polly, how I waited for you to come up to make your witness to Him this evening – but the timing is in His hands, I know, "In my hour shall I seek mine own." Will you join us for refreshments?' he added on a more pragmatic note. 'Your husband has left.'

Polly was stupefied. He thought she was here this evening because she was coming round to the Followers' way of thinking! She had been planning how to join them, how to fake a change of heart, and here was half her work done for her: Drogue already believed she was on the path to salvation! But there was no time now to exploit the situation. It didn't seem so likely now that they'd kidnapped Muffy, but she must get home and find out, she couldn't delay here. And yet to let the opportunity slip was ridiculous.

Inspiration struck. She smiled at Drogue, teeth just showing, eyes half-closed, the smile that had graced so many magazine covers. 'I've got to go now – but could I take one of your books with me?'

Delighted, diverted, Drogue turned on the harsh overhead lights and started rummaging through the boxes. After half a minute he emerged with a triumphant smile. 'Polly, God put my hand on the very work I would have chosen. This is a book I wrote some years ago – the product of my youth, just as my study of Revelations will be the product of Christian maturity. But its message is still as alive today. It is a simple guide to the first steps along the Christian path, especially prepared for baby Christians, as we call them.'

'And would you – would you sign it for me?' She smiled again. He brushed against her as he pulled an alarmingly large pen from his pocket and reached across to press on the desk. Polly took a cursory glance at the cover, which bore a photograph of Drogue not unlike the one she had first seen on the front of *Christian Businessman*. How long ago that seemed.

'Thank you so much – I shall read it – study it – with pleasure.'

'With pleasure, I hope, Polly, but also with profit – spiritual profit, that is.' He put his arm around her; was he going to try to kiss her? Voices were approaching – she disengaged herself and, still smiling, backed towards the door, slipped out and hurried down the stairs.

Outside, free of the maze of concrete service staircases, she breathed in the metallic London air with its summer scents. She pulled the scarf off and shook her hair out. She dragged Drogue's book from her bag and threw it into a litter bin – then, remembering her new purpose, walked back to fish it out. Still brushing crisps off it, she found a taxi.

The lights were on back at the flat; Polly's heart was thumping with mixed fury and fear as she opened the door. Muffy and Francie, side by side on the sofa, were eating chips off a piece of newspaper, transfixed by a programme about bats. Polly strode across and switched off the television.

'Hey, what are you doing? Those little ones are so sweet! Would you believe it, the father suckles the young sometimes? Catch Dad! Switch it on, Mum, do.'

'Where the hell did you both get to? I was waiting for you.' She could hardly tell them of her fears, it would sound so ridiculous.

'We did wait for you at the door, honestly, Mum, then we saw the Followers from Cottenham coming, I was certain they'd recognise me. We went to wait down the hall, and Francie saw this room all laid up for a buffet . . .'

'They had the lot!' Francie burst in. 'Smoked oysters, caviar, huge prawns, champagne . . .'

'You don't mean to say you ate some?'

'Well, the door was open, and we were starving – you told us to join in, and all that singing and waving your arms doesn't half make you hungry. We had a bite, and a glass of the champagne, then we heard them coming – and when we got out, you'd gone.'

'Looking for you – honestly, Muffy, you could have done better.'

'We were fine, but how about you? What on earth is that book, you didn't buy it, did you?'

Muffy reached out for it, but Polly put it back in her bag. She hadn't yet told Muffy that she seriously planned to join the Followers, and now, with Francie here, was not the time. But she would have to tell her soon, because she had the feeling that from now on, things would move quite fast.

Drogue telephoned her two days later. For a panicky moment she wondered whether she'd done the right thing. There was clearly no backing out.

'I hope I'm not disturbing you. I was overjoyed to be able to signal to our group at all levels the positive aspects of your new attitude. We feel that a further meeting would be appropriate; perhaps you would care to lunch with me prior to an informal session with myself and some of my colleagues?'

As Polly put the phone down, all the questions flooded back into her mind. And why were they suddenly so eager to sign her up?

But at least if they were focusing on her, they would leave Muffy alone. By the time she was to meet Drogue for lunch, she was resolved to play her part. She would not only beat them, she would extinguish the lot of them, first the Followers, then their masters, whoever they were.

She was bidden to meet Drogue in one of the newer Knightsbridge hotels. Its excellent restaurant served traditional English food, which she loved; Drogue, somewhat to her surprise, ordered with flair. He asked her about herself; but his rather obvious attempts to draw her out were met by Polly's modestly downcast eyes as she told him about her earlier life, carefully glossing over the wilder moments in her twenties.

'So you were never introduced to the Lord in your infancy?'

'Well, no – my father wasn't interested, and my mother didn't believe in God.' True, though Pauline had become an assiduous churchgoer whenever it suited her purposes.

'It is as I feared,' he said, putting his hand over hers on the table, 'you are one of the many who, like the pagans of early times, have had little chance to meet the Lord. And it is to such as you, after all, that we have been sent to minister, that you may walk in newness of life. Polly, few are chosen, but it is felt that you are one of those destined for redemption, for great works for Christ – do you feel this too?'

Polly wondered if the excellent bottle of claret they had shared hadn't contributed to the warmth of his expression. She smiled her assent, then ventured a question:

'Could I ask – who is it who thinks so well of me?' But Drogue leant back in his chair, smiling in his turn. 'You will learn in the fullness of time, if the Lord so decrees.'

The meeting that followed was held in one of the hotel's private rooms – certainly these people spared no expense. None of the faces were familiar; maybe Drogue was sparing her the presence of Sandra. They were all men, which alarmed Polly only in that she was aware that her instinctive desire to please would be to the fore; she knew she mustn't flirt.

In fact this turned out to be the least of her temptations; chiefly, she wanted to giggle. Somehow she managed to answer their questions, patronising and personal, demurely, humbly; somehow she managed to raise her arms for the prayers with which they concluded:

'O Lord, look upon your backsliding daughter Polly, take pity on her weaknesses. She has followed the world's evil way: forgive her her sins, bring her to new life in You . . .'

At last she was out in the street; she had passed the test, her future with the Followers was mapped out! First, there would be a period of induction in a 'quiet house' they owned; at least it couldn't be Cottenham, with the noise they made there. And then they would 'assess' her. 'We will measure the level of your response to the Lord Jesus. We feel, Polly, that with enablement you may demonstrate management abilities which can be placed in the service of Christ.'

Polly smiled as she made her way along the crowded Knightsbridge pavement. Management abilities! She, Polly, who had never even looked at a bank statement! Well, if they wanted to believe it, let them; it was a step in the right direction.

CHAPTER 13

Two weeks later Polly was pacing up and down her tiny room – a real nun's cell, furnished only with a virginal bed, table, chair and cupboard. She'd known nothing like it since she'd left her boarding school. The huge red-brick house, set in rolling countryside outside Bristol, had been built in the last years of the nineteenth century as a monument to the grandeur of a shipping magnate; now the drawing-room, like Polly's own at Cottenham, was used for worship, the mighty sweep of the staircase ended in a clutter of plastic chairs and tables where coffee and biscuits were served.

Letters in and out were censored – Polly could at least pretend to herself that Edward might have written – and the only papers available were the *Church of England Newspaper, Christianity Today, Gospel News*. Television and radio were forbidden to the inmates, though she had heard a cheery burst of music from the kitchen. Even her pretty dolphin tapestry, which she had hoped to be able to work on, had been taken away from her as unsuitably secular.

This morning, two letters for her had got through the censors – she had given the address out to everyone she could trust, knowing how desperate she'd be for diversion, a taste of the outside world. She could see that neither was from Edward or Jessica, but before she could open them she was swept away with: 'We prefer our junior witnesses to be involved in group activities, Polly. Why don't you work with Pam and Steve on the wall-hanging we're making for the chapel?'

Polly had already seen the appliqué wall-hanging: a number of bloated pink abstract figures, a few token black and yellowish ones among them, making their way towards a lurid central patch of green. She had no idea what it represented, and she hadn't liked to ask. Still, she dutifully sought out Steve, a stocky, crew-cut young man with tattoos up to the elbow – and beyond, for all Polly knew – and found him in the brightly lit rest-room, hunched over a cup of coffee.

'Yeah,' he said, 'do come along – we could do with a bit of company.' He gave her a pleasant grin. He had a surprisingly intelligent face for a Follower, Polly thought, and she was visited again by a feeling she'd had on a couple of other occasions – that she'd met him somewhere before. Certainly not at Cottenham. Where, then? She couldn't think.

The wall-hanging lay on what had once been a magnificent oak table in the main dining-room – now a large empty space, dreary and cold even at the end of May. Pam, an eager, bouncing girl who, as Polly had already noticed, favoured pastel velour tracksuits, was already at work.

'Steve,' she called gaily as they came in, 'don't you feel you need a little – just a little – more movement along the figures? After all, they are running to catch a glimpse of Jesus. Just imagine what it would feel like if we could have that chance. I could show you what I mean,' she added, looking hopefully up at them. Polly bent her head over the wall-hanging, as if fascinated by it, and pretended not to hear. Steve twitched angrily at a corner of it, and – to Polly's surprise – seemed to snarl.

Polly was soon set to pinning a cloud carefully into place. They worked almost in silence until eleven fifteen, when Polly modestly declined Steve's invitation to go with them for a coffee, and as soon as they were out of the room, attacked her letters.

The first one was from Robert. She had never had a letter from Robert before; at least his writing was clear, but it was hard to grasp what he was saying. It was only halfway down the second page, after she'd taken in his profuse apologies, that she realised he was telling her that he'd fallen in love with Alison. Alison? Who on earth was Alison? Of course, the vicar's daughter, the girl they'd taken to the ball. They were going to get married almost immediately. Robert was sure Polly would understand. After a moment or two of rage and sorrow, she did – Robert could hardly be asked to wait indefinitely for a girl who'd disappeared into thin air. She'd never felt entirely happy about his vague engagement to Jessica, his suitability as a husband for her. But his defection somehow set the seal on the breakdown of their lives, made Jessica seem even more hopelessly far away. Polly wiped her face furiously on a corner of the wall-hanging; she'd write to him later, try not to blame him.

The second letter was from Felicity – how had she failed to recognise that unmistakable hand? On a yellowing sheet of finest vellum Felicity had written: 'Polly dear, Smite them hip and thigh (Judges, XV,8) Love and blessings, Felicity.'

A grin stole over Polly's tear-stained face. She would, too. When the time was right.

At least those letters broke the dreary monotony of the days, which Polly found ever harder to bear. The mornings, after a lengthy session of worship, were given up to a series of lectures, discussions, group therapy; the afternoons were devoted to 're-creation', the evenings to Bible study. In the afternoons Polly would skulk in her room to try to avoid the possibility of an outing with her fellow witnesses – 'We do feel everyone should join in, Polly' – and at night would fall exhausted into bed, tired not only by the day's activities but by the constant need to dissimulate.

Never mind, it was working; she was taking them in! That was the main thing. And the knowledge that she was steadily working her way into the Followers' organisation, just as she intended, made it all worthwhile and helped her through many a tedious hour. In the third week she had a brief visit from Jim Drogue:

'Polly, you are showing a very considerable aptitude for your studies; I hear your attitudes are already much improved, and that, while you still show some unfamiliarity with the ways of the Lord, you are making daily progress. However, I understand you are still averse to sharing your time with others; this needs correction. We are all part of one body, Polly, and must act as one. I hope you will bear this in mind.'

When he had gone she did a little dance of triumph round her cell, hugging herself with glee.

She did join some of the outings after that, and on one of the country walks she and quite an attractive man called Alan seemed to fall behind the others, and ended up playing darts in a pub.

They were late for supper; the rest of the group stared at them coldly. But Polly was learning. While Alan did nothing more than mumble an apology, she, with head meekly bowed, asked Pam, her neighbour, if she would repeat grace for her; this done, she gave them an account of the 'quiet time' she had found with Our Lord in the open air. Heads nodding approval, they picked up their soup spoons again. Polly had passed a test.

But the cost! In her little cell, she sometimes thought she would go mad with the boredom and the strain. She missed them all; Edward, with a fierce physical longing, the girls, Harry – and Ruth. She'd managed to visit Ruth again, terrifyingly pale and thin; there was the possibility of another operation, but for the moment they were giving her intensive chemotherapy, her hair was falling out in handfuls.

A thousand times, she questioned what she was doing. It was not yet certain that she would be accepted as a Follower, and if she was, what then? The only thing she'd managed to find out so far was that the organisation was a complete dictatorship. If they did accept her, if she qualified, she'd be assigned a particular task in a particular place; there would be no appeal, no argument. It could be years before she was in a position to decide her own movements – meanwhile she could find herself in the States, even in Russia, like Edward. What could she possibly do, in an alien environment like that, to damage the Followers? Even supposing she was sent somewhere nearer home, did she in fact have any real plans?

Drogue reappeared the following week – Polly's course was finishing, and he had come with a team to make an assessment of the trainees.

The days that followed tested all Polly's patience, all her powers. The role-play intensified: under the watchful eyes of two women, one American, one she thought she remembered as a visitor to

Cottenham, Polly had to sit through a number of 'situational tests'. She felt she wasn't doing too well, but she remembered her lessons and managed to answer briefly and, she hoped, correctly. She was walked through a 'conversion situation' – Drogue himself played the part of the unbeliever, with some ability.

'So who is this Jesus?'

'He is the Lord of us all, the Son of God, the only way to truth and salvation,' Polly replied.

'If he's so powerful, how come he got himself killed?'

'He died willingly, to atone for our sins.' How like the Catholic catechism this was . . .

She was tested on her knowledge of the Bible, and here she starred. She'd never looked at it properly before coming here – snatches were familiar from the readings at the convent, but the gospels were new to her. Such a jumble of the everyday and the extraordinary had to be somewhere near the truth; the directness, let alone the oddness of what Jesus seemed to be saying, reached out across the centuries. She'd suddenly remembered a visit to Venice. She'd longed for an hour away from the friends with whom they were sharing the palazzo; in St Mark's, marvelling at the static golden beauty of the fossilised mosaic figures on the ceiling, her eye had been caught by one small, vivid scene – Christ, urgently pulling some prone figure to his feet. She'd known then that He was everything he said he was. She longed to tell the assessors about this, but it wasn't what they wanted to hear. Their beliefs had nothing to do with that moment of revelation.

The atmosphere among the group was by now quite cheerful. A number of the candidates had already been told that they would be admitted as Followers. On the final Sunday the worship session was led by Drogue. Polly, by now feeling quite friendly towards her fellow inmates – even Pam wasn't a bad old thing, she'd lent her a Tampax when she needed one – sang along with them in the great drawing-room, the now completed hanging staring down at them from the wall. Polly hadn't got much beyond her cloud, sailing rather crookedly across a brilliant blue sky.

Next on the agenda would be lunch – it would be overdone roast beef again, quite reasonable Yorkshire pudding.

As they were filing out of the drawing-room, Alan materialised at her shoulder. 'I've got a bottle of vermouth in my room,' he said out of the corner of his mouth. 'And there's half an hour till lunch.'

'Sounds nice,' said Polly, and followed him up the stairs. What was she doing, jeopardising her chances like this at the very last minute?

'Just keep the Bible handy in case anyone comes in!' Alan said, as she shut the door behind them and he bent to pull a bottle and two glasses out from under his bed. 'I say, did you see that chap someone had smuggled onto the wall-hanging?'

'No, tell me.'

'Mm, a small, naked and very evidently male figure in the bottom left-hand corner. I wondered if you'd done it?'

Polly rolled the first delicious mouthful of vermouth across her tongue. Were there other subversives here, then, besides herself and Alan?

There was a discreet knock on the door. Immediately Polly grabbed the glasses and pushed them back under the edge of the bed. By the time Alan opened the door, she was studiously turning the pages of *Ways to Glory: 100 tips for new Christians*, one of Charles B. Dillet's bestsellers.

'This is very good – I'd like a copy of my own, but can I borrow it for now? Oh – ' She looked up, all innocent surprise to see Jim Drogue in the doorway.

'Ah, Polly, I was told I might find you here. Can you spare me a moment?'

She followed him down the corridor to a room she hadn't been in before; a small study with a view out towards the hills. Something about its proportions reminded her painfully of her little parlour at Cottenham. All the others had already been told whether or not they were fit to become Followers. She hugged her arms around herself. At the worst, he was going to tell her that he'd found her out, that he knew she was a fraud – though she supposed she could just have failed; either way, the last few weeks would have been a waste of time, and she would be no nearer her goal. A flock of rooks, disturbed in one of the trees, flew squawking across the sky.

'We have been watching you carefully, Polly – you are, after all, a very special case. The results of our assessment are on the whole positive. Your written work on Biblical knowledge was particularly well received and showed a thorough knowledge, although your interpretation is unformed as yet. That will change – we shall be sending you on further short courses in the later stages of your Christian development.'

So she'd passed – Polly replaced the ridiculous grin that was about to cover her face with a modest smile.

'But – and now we come to the "buts", Polly – there is a general feeling among both the observation team here at the Centre, and among the assessors, that you have not yet been able fully to integrate yourself with the group life that is so essentially a part of Christianity. Christ himself bade his disciples go forth in twos and threes – in today's wider world, with the challenges we face, we need to unite even more closely against the enemy. There have been signs that you have found it hard to mingle, to join in, and this tendency must be stamped out, Polly, if we are fully to realise the potential you have as a Christian and as a Follower.

'It is pride that is holding you back. Pride, Polly, one of the most grievous of all sins, and we want to help you cast it aside . . .'

The rooks had flown back into the tree now: a group of them were quarrelling ferociously among the leafy branches. Below, she saw two drooping middle-aged women push their bags into a battered Morris Minor and climb in: she knew they'd failed the assessment, probably they couldn't face lunch with the new Followers. But she must concentrate. Drogue was still droning on:

'We have made a plan which will both test your true vocation as a Follower, and heal, with Christ's help, those wounds which pride is inflicting on your soul. As you are aware, Sandra, one of our most trusty founder members, is in charge of your old home – ' he glanced at a note on his desk ' – at Cottenham House. We are sending you there to be under her surveillance, to humble yourself amidst the scenes of your more worldly life. Now Polly, let us pray together.'

*

Rather grudgingly, he gave her a week's grace.

'Polly, the Lord does not wait upon us – rather we should wait upon Him. I had hoped your new calling would be signalled by a readiness to enter eagerly into His service. What do you need the time for?'

'For prayer and reflection,' Polly ad libbed. 'Perhaps you could recommend me some books which would help me?' She could hardly tell him that if she had to embark on the next stage of her Christian life without a breather, she thought she might go mad. Besides, she must see Muffy and tell her what was happening.

Drogue graciously nodded. 'By the way, Polly,' he said, 'there's something I've been meaning to ask you. I believe Edward said you own a château in France, near Riberac. Is that right?'

'Yes.' A wave of misery suddenly engulfed Polly as she remembered their last visit; the heat of summer on the slopes of the great hills around, the big living-room fragrant with that unidentifiable French smell – damp stone, woodsmoke, pot pourri.

'How big is it?' Drogue asked.

'Ten – no, eleven bedrooms, if you count the little one in the tower.'

Drogue beamed approvingly. 'It does sound as if it might make an excellent base for the Followers in France. There is so much work for the Lord to do there, Polly. Perhaps you could compile a report for me on the suitability of the house as a centre for the Followers, and on Christian feeling in the area generally.'

The idea of it! She could just see how well the Followers would go down with the locals in their village – and, since she and Edward had deliberately chosen an isolated part of the country, it was hardly a good place from which to start a mass conversion of the French!

As she reached the door, Drogue called her back. 'One more question, Polly – how is your sick friend?'

'She's just had another operation.' Polly answered him shortly, for Drogue had only glimpsed Ruth that one time at the ball; why this concern? But he seemed determined not to let the matter rest.

'When you see her, tell her that we are praying for her, and that we have plans to translate our prayer into action. The Lord is the source of many wonders, Polly; great is his hand.'

Polly, whose mind had drifted away to poor Ruth, smiled vaguely and left the room.

CHAPTER 14

Adrian met Polly at the station; he was easily recognisable, as he never appeared to change his clothes at all – or perhaps he had lots, exactly the same? The Aran sweater and the beige cords were in place, as were the open-toed sandals.

He greeted her quite affably, though he seemed a little diffident as he saw her into her own Volvo. She hardly minded; she'd never had any feeling for cars, they were indistinguishable and interchangeable as far as she was concerned, and she was too nervous at the thought of seeing Cottenham again to think about anything else. But she managed to chatter brightly all the way there, asking after the various members of the group – she only paused when they reached the village.

'The shop – it's closed down!' Though she'd visited it infrequently herself, the girls had always spent their pocket-money there on sweets; while more and more of the locals bought their main supplies in Woodbridge, you could find almost anything at Hibbert's and, with its irregular opening hours, it was a godsend for last-minute things.

'Yes – we hadn't realised that they were opening on Sundays!' Adrian turned shocked eyes on Polly, narrowly missing the gatepost as they turned into the Cottenham drive. 'I went first and spoke to Mr Hibbert myself; I tried to change his mind, but he seemed to find it difficult to see our point of view. After some prayer and thought, we managed to persuade him of his wrongdoing. We're thinking of buying the building to use as an information centre and Christian outlet.'

He was parking now, and Polly looked around her, horrified. They'd cut down the big old chestnut at the bottom of the lawn, where the girls had had their swing, and the tulip tree nearer the house which cast a shade for tea in summer. Of course the little lead statue that had stood in front of the dense rhododendron bushes was gone; in its place a gigantic wooden crucifix towered above a new concrete terrace. They'd dug up the roses which had surrounded the sweep of the gravel forecourt, and tarmacked over the whole area.

'Has Edward seen this?' she asked.

Adrian had observed her looking around; he'd regained his confidence after the gatepost. 'Oh yes. Now, we put the cross there so that we can worship in the open air. Meg usually leads the prayers there; you remember Meg, don't you?'

'Yes,' Polly replied faintly – those lovely trees would never grow again – 'I remember her being a real outdoor girl.' Had she said the right thing? Adrian smiled approvingly.

'Well, Bart's been in charge in the garden; he's made a few changes for the better, cleared it a bit. Then Sandra had some good suggestions for the house – it's a bit easier to run now, she says; and you'll be glad of that, Polly, now you'll be working alongside us.' He looked dubiously at her Vuitton suitcase, at her clothes. She had changed into the simplest things she had, dark grey culottes, a tawny crew-necked sweater; obviously designed to be seen rather than used, they clearly didn't please him.

There was the sound of a concrete-mixer from the back of the house. The hall was unaltered, though the furniture was gone.

'We'd have liked to take that out,' Adrian gestured towards the beautiful sweep of the oak staircase. 'We could use the room it takes up. Unfortunately there's a preservation order. Still, we're doing what we can,' he said cheerily. 'Luckily, one of the chaps on the Council is a Christian, so we're hopeful. Sorry about the racket – they're screeding over those old stone floors at the back. Then we'll get some vinyl tiles down – it'll be much easier to clean, as you'll find out. We found some good people to do it, they're all believers, you can be sure, so God is speeding their hand. We're cooking in the dining-room at the moment – we took out that old fireplace so that we could fit some units in for the time being, until we get a proper modern kitchen fitted.' He turned. 'Hello, Sandra, I've got her safe and sound.'

Sandra stood at the foot of the stairs, head thrown back, arms extended towards Polly in a rather theatrical gesture.

'Welcome, Polly. Welcome in the name of Christ!' Polly flinched slightly as she was embraced, but managed to keep on her face the half-smile she'd worn since the house had come into sight.

'Polly, we hear good things of you,' Sandra said as she guided her up the stairs, 'good tidings. Your signs of repentance, your turning toward the Lord, are surely a cause for great rejoicing. "Truly, the sheep that was lost is found, and we should be glad in our hearts." We've arranged a little celebration for this evening. No, not in there.' Polly had automatically turned towards her old bedroom – her bedroom and Edward's. 'We must be new in all our ways!' Sandra continued playfully, as she led her up to the top floor.

Here, more builders were visible; Polly thought she caught a glimpse of a colourful magazine tucked away as the younger of the two men put down his mug and went to help his colleague manoeuvre a sheet of plasterboard into position. The three bigger attics were being subdivided, Sandra explained, to house the growing numbers of Followers.

'Just until we finish the extension. Dean designed that – it was surely part of God's plan that we should find such a good architect among us. We do indeed have a diversity of gifts around here, and we like to share our talents – that's what Christianity is all about, as you'll find, Polly.' Dean – wasn't he the one whose cache of bottles Muffy had found up here? Polly wondered where he kept them now.

Sandra pushed open an ill-fitting door. 'You'll be in good company up here, Polly. Now, prayers at six, supper at six forty-five, then we'll celebrate your return to the fold. There are thirty of us, so we can praise the Lord in style. I'm going to let you off your duties today, Polly; we'll have a talk later, and I can outline my plans – our plans, I should say, God's and ours – for you then. And we'll find you something more suitable to wear.'

After the prayers, the really quite adequate supper – fresh vegetables from the Cottenham kitchen gardens – and the sing-song which followed, Polly was beckoned into a room with Sandra's name on the door. It was her own little sitting-room, the pictures gone, the worn, pretty Chinese rug still in place! Sandra's earlier affability had disappeared; her smile was cool as she faced Polly across the desk.

'As I said, Polly, we are glad to have you here – and so glad that you are on the path to redemption. But I must be straight with you. Your report indicates that there is still room for improvement; that there is a residue of hardness of heart, of stubborn wilfulness – above all, of pride – that must be rooted out.' How much better she'd looked in glasses, Polly thought; contact lenses only showed up the small size and nondescript colour of her eyes.

'We like to deal with new Followers on a one-to-one basis, and you will be in my charge, Polly.' Sandra smiled with some relish. 'I shall be looking for the signs of the Spirit working in you – for fellowship, for joy, and particularly for obedience.'

When it was over, Polly collapsed onto the bed in her room – a room no bigger than the cell at the Followers' Centre she had just left. The new partition walls were thin, and she could hear someone scratching around next door – finally, after an alarming fit of coughing, her neighbour was silent.

Sandra had explained the structure to her. She had the committee working under her – Adrian, Meg, Paul, Judith and Bethany. Cottenham functioned basically as a training-centre for Christian mission. Groups of twenty to thirty men and women would spend up to three months being prepared to go out into the world and spread the word. There was a distinct hierarchy; the lower-level candidates would be given a basic training, others would be groomed to take over further 'cells' of the Followers' activity.

Polly had waited hopefully for more information on the upper echelons of the Follower structure, but it was clear that none would be forthcoming. 'We don't find it necessary for our more junior witnesses to have contact with anything above their immediate superiors,' Sandra said, and added, 'Curiosity is not encouraged –

"each to his own part".' Had she noticed Polly's eyes wandering to the grey filing cabinets across the desk? Certainly, she gathered up the papers lying there with a dismissive nod.

'Polly, service has to be part of our calling – the service of others. We're not sure if you're advanced far enough along this path. So we're going to test you out by asking you to serve us, the committee, as we serve God. For the first month or so we'll be looking to you to support us in all our activities . . .'

She was going to be a maid-of-all-work in her own home.

Polly got up off the bed and went to the small window. Here, the ghostly grey of the foundations of the new extension had replaced her formal garden; a few pitiable remnants of the box hedges stood to one side. She had only to look at them, to look at the new partition walls that enclosed her, to think of the desecration of her beautiful roses, those trees, for her flagging resolve to return. Luck had been with her in her return to Cottenham; now that she was here, on her own territory, she would make plans, start to take some action. What it would be, she didn't yet know – but even if she had to strangle all the Followers one by one, with her own hands, somehow she would get Cottenham back and make it beautiful again.

It took her almost a month to get established, weeks of shattering hard work, and of such intense identification with the Followers that she wondered, at times, whether she wasn't herself being taken over. She scrubbed, she dusted, she fetched and carried. She sang along with the hymns in her harsh soprano; she started guitar lessons with Judy so that she could take a more active part in the worship. At the morning and evening sessions nobody prayed more loudly or fervently than she did; she discovered a gift for extemporary prayer – much admired by the Followers, though she was rather frightened by it. And at the weekly 'discipling' sessions she was always full of ideas for projects.

It was at one of these sessions that Polly made her first move.

The subject of discussion that morning was the cellars; the Followers were wishing they could use them to store some of the unwanted Cottenham furniture but unfortunately most of the cellarage was occupied by Edward's large store of wine, and although the Followers had wanted it simply tipped away, Jim Drogue had given strict instructions that it should be left.

Polly suddenly had an idea. 'The wine needn't take up nearly as much space as it does, though,' she said earnestly, breaking into the conversation. 'It just needs someone to go down there and shove all the racks up together, pile all the cases up – then there'd be lots of room.' She looked around at them with a meek Christian smile. 'Someone strong. Like you, Dean.'

Dean volunteered for the job at once – and Polly smiled again; but this time it was an inward smile that she didn't let anybody see.

A week later the discussion was about the young, and the need to evangelise. 'Why doesn't Bart – ' Bart was an ex-teacher ' – go round the playgrounds?' Polly suggested. At least it would cut down on the time he spent tearing up her garden – but she couldn't really believe they'd be naive enough to send him off to wander round the local school playgrounds talking about Jesus.

They did, though. And Polly felt she could sit back for a bit, and see if her ideas bore fruit.

A few days later, Jim Drogue visited Cottenham; Sandra called Polly into her office. 'Jim has made special arrangements to show you the Lord's work in action, Polly. You are privileged. You are excused afternoon duties; be ready at two o'clock.'

Intrigued, and just a bit apprehensive, Polly appeared in the hall after lunch to find a little group already assembled: Drogue, Adrian, Sandra and Meg. Drogue beamed at her. 'Ah, Polly. Now our party is complete. Come with us to witness the dynamic power of our Lord and Saviour.'

Drogue drove them, in Edward's Mercedes; Polly sat between Meg and Sandra in the back. It was only when they drew up outside the hospital in Ipswich that, with a sickening lurch of the heart, she understood. Ruth!

'I want you just to observe, Polly,' Drogue said as the five of them tramped down the long corridor to Ruth's ward. 'Take a back seat; watch and pray while we minister to your sick friend.'

Why didn't somebody stop them? Polly asked herself wildly, looking round. Surely they couldn't all be allowed just to march in like this? There seemed to be only one nurse on duty at the reception desk; a West Indian woman. As they approached, she stood up, beaming. 'Good to see you, Mr Drogue. Just go right in now, and do your healing work.'

Ruth had been moved from the six-bedded ward into a single room. She lay in the bed, thin and balding; her hands, imprisoned by drips and bandages, rested on the sheet. She looked so weak and ill; Polly could hardly bear it. The five of them seemed to loom like giants in the room. She hung back, angry, ashamed and helpless.

Ruth turned her head slowly to look at them. She probably recognised Drogue and Sandra from the ball at The Gunnocks, Polly thought. 'I'm afraid it isn't visiting hours, you know,' she said weakly. 'I've just had an operation, I'm very tired and I want to sleep.'

'We shall not detain you long,' Drogue said. 'I am aware of your condition and it is that which has brought me here.'

Ruth was barely audible. 'I'm sorry, but I'd really rather you went.'

Adrian spoke. 'Ruth, we feel that we have been directed here to carry out a special part of our mission. First we want you to accept this.' He laid a brightly bound hardback book on her bedside table; *The Glad Tidings Bible*, the cover proclaimed. 'Then we want to bring the power of Christ to bear upon you. We are going to ask Jim to place his hands upon you and to exercise his gift of healing.' Adrian stood aside and beckoned Jim Drogue forwards with a rather melodramatic gesture. The others bowed their heads. Polly saw that, somehow, Ruth was managing to reach the bedside bell and press it.

'I'm afraid Christ doesn't mean very much to me,' Ruth said. 'I'm Jewish. And I want you to go.'

The nurse's face looked round the door, still beaming. 'Everything all right then, Mrs Harding? You're lucky to have this fine man Mr Drogue come and visit you! It's good to see the Spirit at work!' She disappeared, and to her horror, Polly saw Drogue advance upon Ruth.

Keep calm, she told herself. They can't actually be doing any harm with this meaningless nonsense. But surely there ought to be something she could do to save her friend from this indignity? If only, by some miracle, Harry would come! Drogue was making movements over Ruth's body with his arms now, murmuring a prayer to which the others made little grunts of assent. Then he put his hands on her forehead; his face loomed over her. His speech changed to a foreign language, but not one that Polly had ever heard – it sounded more like a child trying to talk, the words were unrecognisable, the sound was varied, very fluent and not unpleasant. Suddenly Polly realised that he was speaking in tongues; out of sheer interest, her anger diminished a little.

Drogue was rounding off his performance with a few more prayers; thank God, they'll go now, Polly thought.

'There's one more thing, and we will make it very brief – but we feel it is essential to your healing. We would like you to accept baptism in the name of our Lord Jesus Christ.'

'No,' said Ruth.

'You are in a weakened state, Ruth. We are guided to know what is best for you, and we beg you willingly to accept what the Lord Christ offers.'

'I said no.' With anguish, Polly heard her friend's voice growing faint. 'I'm Jewish. I don't practise, but my people and their way of life are important to me. I don't want to be baptised.'

'Come, Ruth, let us lead you to salvation.' Drogue was approaching her again. Her voice rose to a thin scream: 'NO!' The door burst open and Harry rushed in, carrying a bottle of champagne and a huge bunch of red roses.

'What are you doing to my wife? Get out of here!'

'You can't talk to Mr Drogue like that!' Adrian was appalled.

'Can't I just?' said Harry. 'And to you too. I know about you lot. Get out!'

'Are you going to make me?'

'Yes.' Polly saw Harry drop the champagne onto a pile of towels, and lunge. Even as he did so, Drogue stepped forward, making conciliatory gestures – the big, solid mass of roses caught him full in the face. Surprised, he lost his balance and tripped backwards against a wheeled table which propelled him across the room to the basin, on which he cracked his head before falling to the floor. Two vases – lilies, iris and carnations – fell from the table onto him – he lay there like Ophelia, almost completely covered with flowers.

Polly watched, transfixed, as, turning, Harry hit Adrian on the side of the chin; he staggered, then recovered, and Harry doubled up as the taller man thumped him in the solar plexus. Meg seemed to be having hysterics; Sandra was kneeling on the floor attending to Drogue.

From her corner, Polly could see that Adrian was about to go for Harry again. She must do something! She started forward – but it was Ruth who, summoning all her strength, picked up the *Glad Tidings Bible* and threw it. The chunky book in its serviceable binding caught Adrian squarely on the head; he lurched, Harry hit him again, and he went down. Harry then slapped Meg hard across the face; the shrieks stopped, it was like switching off a toy. Silence fell, broken only by the muffled sound of a television in the next room, and the water dripping from one of the vases.

'Oh Ruth, those lovely roses – still, the champagne's intact.'

It was all over; a patient down the corridor, alarmed by Meg's screams, had alerted the ward sister, who arrived with a posse of nurses. The two men had been assisted down to the casualty department amid much banter ('Well, at least you got into trouble in the right place'): Sandra and Meg had gone with them, and Polly was snatching a few moments alone with Harry and Ruth.

'So's Harry,' Ruth said, smiling. 'You fought like a tiger, darling – and you've never hit anyone, have you? Do you remember how I used to think you ought to smack Dave sometimes, and you couldn't?'

They gazed lovingly at one another, and Polly had to look away, a lump in her throat. When she looked back at Ruth, she found herself doing a sort of double-take. 'Ruth, you look better. I mean, better even than when we first came in.' Her cheeks were faintly pink, her skin looked healthier.

Ruth thought about it. 'Yes, I feel fine. All that excitement must have done me good!' She looked with concern at Polly. 'But how are you? At least you'll have some money now, won't you?'

'What do you mean?'

'Oh Polly, didn't you know? Edward's sold the business – it was in the papers.'

CHAPTER 15

It was exactly a week later that the first of Polly's schemes came to fruition: Dean was found unconscious in the cellars. The following morning he was taken away in disgrace to a Christian centre for alcoholics.

This was generally dismissed as an unfortunate incident, but it visibly shook Sandra's confidence. For the first weeks she'd taken great delight in giving Polly all the dreariest jobs around the place, but now she seemed to be swayed by the good opinion of the Followers. It was clear to Polly that, underneath the henna rinse, the new clothes, lay the same insecurity and longing to cling – Sandra needed a mentor, a boss, as much as she ever had. And what was more likely, Polly thought, than that, in spite of everything, she should turn back to her old one?

Gradually Sandra relaxed with her; she began to trust this new, humble Polly. Why shouldn't she? Her mind worked quite simply. Polly had never bothered to dissemble with her in their previous life together, so Sandra assumed that she was genuine now, and called her quite frequently into the sitting-room to 'share'. Group members were encouraged to spy on each other; Polly, whose whole soul was against the concept of sneaking, had no qualms when it came to Bethany, the next to go.

The time when her two little boys had been caught reading the *Beano* was already a black mark against the family; Bethany was on probation, and Sandra had confessed to some doubts about her.

'Polly – Bethany was absent from the group session this morning.

I'm not too happy about her attitude at present. Keep an eye on her for me, would you? We need to guard against any backsliding – and it will be a good test of your new Christian alertness.'

It was only a matter of days before Polly, wearily dusting round the landing – the builders, Christian or not, made a fantastic mess and seemed unlikely to finish, ever – caught a glimpse through the open door of Bethany's room. Bethany was curled up on her bed with a paperback Jackie Collins. As Polly strode in to confront her, she pushed it under the pillow, flushing guiltily.

'You won't tell, will you?' she begged.

'I'll have to, won't I?' Polly had never felt worse, but the memory of her own empty bookshelves at Connaught Square, swept clear of books by the Followers, strengthened her.

'Please – they might turn me out, and where would I go, with the boys?' Bethany was crying now.

'You can take them back to their father.' They'd be much better off out of the place. Bethany's desperate red face, her tears, drove Polly to real cruelty. She pulled the book out from under the pillow. 'Where would you go, indeed,' she hissed. 'What do you think I felt like when you turned me out of here? When you threw my books out?'

Bethany was bawling loudly now; the commotion drew not only her older boy into the room, but Sandra herself. Her eyes flew to Polly, then to the paperback. Her mouth tightened.

'It's all right,' chirped little Joshua. 'Mummy's read that – I expect she wouldn't mind lending it.' Their fate was sealed.

As they left next morning, Polly managed to slip the boys a fiver each – gratitude, guilt – under cover of a commotion in the hall. Sandra, flushed, seemed to be having a confrontation with a young couple; the husband hung back, but the wife was shouting:

'Getting hold of my Ryan like that when he came out of school, giving him sweets – we know about his type . . .'

Polly's heart gave a lurch of triumph. Sandra, still in control, said: 'Just a minute, I'm sure we can sort this out, what did you say your name was?' She took Polly by the arm. 'Fetch Bart, will you, these two think he's been, ah, interfering with their son down at the primary.'

As Polly hastened away, the mother's voice was raised again: 'I've told the Head, I've half a mind to go to the police . . .'

Later, still glowing with secret triumph, Polly went into the village; it was her turn to go to the post box. Usually she dreaded this. Since her return, when a surprised Mrs Hibbert had spotted her in the street, she'd felt almost tangible waves of hostility every time she went down there. She could hardly explain why she'd joined the Followers, and the locals quite reasonably supposed that its members were at Cottenham at her instigation. Still, perhaps today she wouldn't see anyone she knew.

But outside the pub, she ran into Mr Hibbert. She didn't have time to feel awkward.

'Oh, Mr Hibbert, I'm so sorry about the shop!' He looked at her grumpily.

'Yes, it was that lot up there – and I still can't believe you're mixed up with them like they say you are, and you so good to the kids always.' Polly did remember taking his son to the hospital once, when his car had broken down. And there'd always been the Christmas party for the village children.

'Well, I'm not exactly – but I can't really tell you about it.' She felt a rush of affection for him; his gloomy bloodhound face and dusty shelves had been part of all their lives for so long. 'But what are you going to do?'

'Find another shop somewhere, I suppose – there's not much going round here, and it's hard to uproot. But I'd like to get even with that lot first, they really put the pressure on me. Got the health inspectors in, then tipped off the VAT. All that about Christianity and prayer, then they do that to me. It was that Meg was the worst.'

She would be, Polly thought – she was vociferous about Sunday observance at all their meetings. Suddenly she had another brilliant idea; didn't they say that success breeds success? She took Hibbert's arm and drew him round the corner of the pub. She spoke quickly and quietly:

'Oh yes, Meg. You know that big cross they've put up in the garden?'

'I do too,' said Hibbert, puzzled. 'Charlie Rose put it up for them, and a rotten job he made of it if you ask me. Never been the worker his father was, has Charlie. Wouldn't give it a chance if we have another gale.'

'Exactly.' Polly looked at him meaningfully. 'Now Meg likes to pray in front of it, every morning at six thirty; she prostrates herself – ' Hibbert looked at her questioningly ' – she lies down on her face in front of it for about twenty minutes. She does it rain or shine, just on time, I couldn't believe it at first.' She paused. 'I've seen that cross swaying in the wind, I get quite worried for her.'

'Ah.' Hibbert nodded, and Polly saw a smile curve his mouth. 'Wouldn't take much to make it a real hazard, that cross.'

'No,' said Polly. 'It wouldn't.'

When it fell, the cross missed its target, as Polly had been almost certain it would. Meg didn't have the heart-attack until she scrambled up and saw it lying inches away from where she had been. Sandra was in her element in the crisis; within seconds she had sent Meredith out with blankets, told Polly to ring for an ambulance, and detailed Adrian to calm the new group of Follower trainees who'd just arrived. Polly took the opportunity to ring not only the ambulance service but the local paper.

The ambulance men were there twenty minutes later, and Meg was carried away. Prayers, which centred around her, were double the usual length, and supper was a subdued affair. It was not until two days later, when a piece appeared in the local press, that Sandra called a meeting of the committee. At the last minute she asked Polly to join them.

'Of course, Meg's welfare is our prime concern – luckily, the attack was a mild one, though she'll be hospitalised for some time – and our prayers are with her. But there are other matters about which we are anxious. We don't yet know how the news of this tragic accident reached the press – we've already had more calls – and you can be sure there will be a full enquiry.' Her pale eyes flickered around the room. 'Worse, there are mutterings of Satanic activity in our midst – several of the newcomers have been heard to interpret the fall of the cross as a sign of the power of the Evil

One in our midst.' There were murmurs of excitement and horror from around the room. 'I feel that this is something which should be dealt with at the highest level; I am therefore preparing to take the unprecedented step of contacting headquarters – with your agreement, that is – and summoning our elders for further discussion.'

Adrian's hand was raised. 'Shouldn't we first make an effort to find the source of evil in our midst?' he asked. Had he glanced at Polly?

'I shall seek guidance on that matter at headquarters,' answered Sandra firmly, and added, 'and in prayer, of course. Now, are we all in favour of my plan?'

That evening was hot and still; a light haze had hung over the countryside all day, shimmering over the river, shrouding the distant hills and copses with heat. Polly knew this weather well; often, in the late summer, the four of them would be at Cottenham on their own, without guests, and spend the long, hot afternoons together in the garden – Edward reading, she gardening, the girls lounging about in big straw hats. Mrs Beamish would bring out tea, then later they'd change for drinks and dinner. Now, as she laid the formica-topped, canteen-style tables in the dining-room, she could almost see the polished oak under the Mason ironstone dinner service she'd found in a saleroom, and Edward's family silver shining among the flowers and candles. How it hurt, to remember.

She took the feed down to the chickens. The hens, with their bright eyes and robot movements, had always amused her, and it was one of the few times when she could be out of doors, alone. As she walked back through the mist into the more familiar part of the garden, the sense of the past was still so strongly with her that, when she saw a man's figure on the other side of the stream, she knew straightaway that it was Edward. She stopped, breathless, and almost immediately conscious of her cropped hair, the blue cotton, shapeless, boiler-suit, the bucket in her hand. Edward, come back to her, come back to rescue her, as she had known he would. She put the bucket down rather carefully, and crossed the little bridge. Then she saw his black hair – it was Toby. He made no move forward; his eyes were fixed on her with an expression in them which she couldn't make out. Anxiety? Tenderness?

'Toby?'

'I've wanted so much to ...' His voice tailed away. 'I've wondered so much how you were managing ...'

Sudden emotion made her voice brisk. 'Have you any news, Toby? D'you know where Jessica is, or when Edward's coming back?'

He stared at her. 'But you know better than I do – aren't you with these people now?'

Of course, he didn't know what she was doing, why should he, and she couldn't explain now. And yet she suddenly so much wanted to, felt how comforting it would be to have him as her ally. He had always been such a good friend to her ... Surely she couldn't be crying? 'Where have you been?' she asked him – the first question that came into her head.

'Around, only I couldn't bear to see the house any more, without you and Edward ... I didn't realise you were here until I spoke to old Hibbert in the pub – he said there'd been a bit of trouble.' He took a step forward, and put his hand out to her awkwardly. 'Polly, if I can help at all – let me know, won't you?'

What was he offering? As he stood there, looking at her so intently, so like Edward, and yet so unlike, she felt –

Inside the house, the bell rang for supper.

'Toby, that's really kind, but everything's all right.'

She wavered, then turned, but not before she had seen the look of disappointment in his eyes.

The atmosphere at Cottenham was strained and anticipatory for the next day or so, though the arrival of the new trainees kept them all busy. Sandra stayed in her office, emerging only to issue orders; several times she called Polly in, it was clear she simply wanted someone to listen to her. In the village things were more cheerful; Polly, as she passed on various Followers' errands, heard some lively carousing in the pub.

One morning, walking back up the drive from the post-box, she saw a new group of cars on the tarmac. Drogue? she wondered, with a slightly sinking heart; she'd been so careful, but it was rather like school – even the thought of him made her feel guilty. But why were there two police cars there as well? She took a path behind the remaining beech tree, where she'd secretly established a new bed for her favourite hostas; as she emerged, she saw Bart being guided into one of two police cars by an officer.

A smile spread over her face. It had worked! The smile disappeared as she noticed Muffy stepping out of the other police car. She hurried towards her.

'Muffy, lovely to see you, what are you doing here?'

'End of term, Mum, just like you to forget. There was no one at the station so I got a lift with those chaps – we can get my luggage tomorrow. Didn't you want me back?' Muffy sounded aggrieved.

'Well, yes, darling, but there's so much going on here. You've only just gone back, these schools are monstrous.'

Muffy ignored her mother's ritual complaint. 'Any news of Jess?'

'Not a word – I can't stop worrying.' One more big dark car was coming up the drive; this time, Polly saw, it really was Drogue. She pulled Muffy aside.

'Now listen, Muffy, we've got to lie low if we're ever going to sort this business out and get Dad and Jessica and the houses back. Please do be good.' She hadn't spoken with that note in her voice for years. Muffy's round yellow eyes took on a suitably serious expression.

'I'll be all right, Mum, I promise – look at me.' Indeed, she was dressed with astonishing conservatism. 'And I'm not going to hang around here getting my bottom pinched by Adrian.' Polly laughed at the very idea. 'I could stay with Toby,' Muffy went on, 'and just come over now and again.' Polly felt the sharp pain of jealousy – Muffy was free to come and go as she pleased. Muffy would have the comfort of being with Toby.

'All right, good idea. Apart from anything else, there's not much room around here. Don't say too much to Toby. I must find out what's going on. Come back tomorrow, and we'll get your things, and talk.'

Muffy kissed her briefly, and pushed through the hedge on her way to the short-cut across the fields.

Drogue had disembarked from the car – he nodded to Polly as she reached the door, and disappeared inside with the others. Another man was getting out; this time it was, heart-stoppingly, unmistakably, Edward. There was no way she could hide herself, disappear – the moment she had longed for, dreaded, had arrived.

'I thought you were in Russia again?' She couldn't think of anything else to say; she heard her own voice pitched rather higher than usual, with a desperate, querying note in it. Edward smiled, the charming smile that had first won her.

'As you see, I'm here.' The others had gone inside. He stretched his hand towards her; out of habit, out of love, she moved until his arm encircled her, and rested her head wearily on his shoulder. It was over, the nightmare time; he'd come to get the house back, to turn these people out, to reclaim her and the girls. Jessica! Now that the answer was so near, she could hardly bear to ask the question. She looked up at him as he moved a pace away; she'd let him speak first.

'It's good to see you, Polly – those clothes suit you!' She laughed, then realised he meant it. Perhaps she did look good in butcher blue, she'd never thought so – and maybe she'd keep her hair short if he liked it that way. 'Polly – it's been so long . . .' He turned his head away a little. 'I had to come back.' He'd always been inarticulate, nearly as wordless as Toby, when he was deeply moved; his mere reappearance had swept away her doubts, but she longed for him to say the magic words, to put his arms right round her, to tell her that they'd all be back together again. He drew a deep breath.

'Polly, I wanted to see whether you'd changed, and it looks as if you have – it sounds as if you have . . .'

How could he think that? 'No, oh no, I haven't – oh Edward, I've missed you so, I've been so miserable . . .'

He turned back to her; now he looked puzzled. Laughing with

relief, happiness, she looked up at him. 'Of course I was miserable without you ... now you're back it'll be all right again, won't it?' The warm, pretty houses, Jessica back with her, the parties, the holidays, Edward there to love and admire and cosset her. She'd sack Sandra, of course, and turn out the Followers, but that would be revenge enough. It would take time to get things back in order, Cottenham might never be quite the same again, but the bad times were over.

'Polly, of course I understand that this time of transition must have been difficult for you; you have to remember that change is often a time of development, of growth.' She stepped back – what was he saying? 'But I hear the best reports of you – Sandra says you've turned from your old ways; your attitudes have improved greatly, that your acceptance, your humility and your supportive qualities have been well to the fore in recent weeks. Jim Drogue is here with me and he's particularly anxious to interview you later – you can rest assured you'll get a warm greeting from him.'

'Sandra – Jim Drogue?' Polly could only stare at him. So he hadn't come back to her; he was still with the Followers. Edward's face had its mask-like look; the white of his hair, his eyes, his normal pallor, blended into the mist behind. Perhaps this was all a dream, he hadn't come at all. She put out a hand to touch him again, to make one last plea. But he spoke first.

'Of course I love you.' Was there still some hope? 'I love you as we are bidden to love all our brothers and sisters in Christ, and I am only too happy to hear of the progress you have been making. Perhaps – as you grow towards God, and seek His forgiveness – it'll be possible for us to make a new start together.' There was a beseeching note in his voice as he looked down at her.

'Where's Jessica?' she asked through dry lips.

He shook his head gently, as if this was a matter of no importance. He was looking at her hopefully. 'Think it over,' he said.

Anger was growing in her now – she could feel her hand on his arm becoming a claw. How dare he destroy the hope he'd just encouraged? Yet some faint part of her almost wanted to give in, to accept the new terms. She looked round her desperately, as if the trees, the walls, could hold some comfort. When she turned back, Edward had gone inside.

She trailed wearily round to the back door; in the passage she found Judy comforting Meredith. As she mounted the stairs, she thought she heard muffled sounds of sobbing from Sandra's room on the first floor – the blue spare room. By this time she had more or less collected herself. She was only back where she had been an hour before, she reasoned – and if her talk with Edward had finally killed all her dreams of a reunion, so much the better. At least she hadn't given herself away.

CHAPTER 16

Just as insurance, and to keep her own spirits up, she changed into one of the good dresses she'd kept, deceptively simple apricot-coloured wool. She hadn't worn it for a while. To her relief, she found out that the visiting party – Drogue, Edward and two American women – were to eat separately; she laid their places demurely. She must somehow find out when Edward was leaving, for how long she would have to endure the torture of seeing him. He hadn't even asked after Muffy. She must keep her away until he was gone.

After prayers, led by Drogue, a message came: could she go to Sandra's office?

Sandra, however, was not in her office when Polly knocked and went in. It was Drogue who awaited her. He looked appreciatively at her dress, at her slim legs as she sat down, demurely crossing them.

'I gather you've already spoken with Edward.'

'Yes.'

'I know it can't have been easy for you, but at least the ice is broken now.' There was a human note in his voice which made her almost like him, in spite of everything. 'I think we're all going to be working very closely together in the future.' He twinkled at her. 'Edward, of course, has to continue his mission in Russia, he'll be giving an informal talk tomorrow on the great work the Lord is doing in that country, then he leaves.' Thank God for that, thought Polly. 'But we have many other plans for you – plans which we can only now reveal in the light of the great – the very great –

advances which the Spirit and the grace of God have made in you. More prayer is indicated, Polly, more prayer to defeat the wiles of Satan which are not yet dead in you . . .'

Polly wondered what was coming. She couldn't stop thinking about Edward. She supposed she should add him to her hit-list. 'And more action,' she heard Drogue say in more businesslike tones.

'We are deeply grieved,' he went on, 'by the events which have occurred among the leadership here; the departure of Bethany, in which your part has received the highest commendation, Dean's sad fall from grace, Meg's accident, the case of Bart; this last seems to be based on a tragic misunderstanding, but is nonetheless a severe setback for our enterprise, a blot on the stainless purity of the banner we should carry as His followers. We must be above reproach, Polly, above reproach if we are to act as an example to others.'

Drogue cleared his throat, and continued: 'We have shared this message with Sandra, and gently indicated to her that we must seek new ways for the time being. You are coming to the fore, Polly, you are the chosen one, and it is upon you that the privilege – and the burden – of the future here must rest for a short while, until we can spare a more fully trained Divisional Director. You will be on trial, Polly, the kind of trial that is the lot of so many Christians . . . A short while ago I would not have believed this would be possible, but the Holy Spirit is full of surprises . . .'

Polly could hardly believe her ears – she was to supplant Sandra, she would be in charge! She could do anything she liked – rip up the tarmac, sack the lot of them, get the garden going again, use the Followers as slave labour to do it! But almost at once, caution came to temper her elation. She'd learnt enough to be very careful. Legally, the Followers had Cottenham for the next ten years. And Jessica, Jessica; if she antagonised them, she might never find her.

'I'm overwhelmed – I shall only hope that I can, with the help of the Spirit, live up to this new challenge. Thank you, Jim, for putting this trust in me.'

'I'm glad of your enthusiasm!' He patted her knee approvingly. 'But don't thank me, thank the Lord who, every time he closes a door, opens a window. Your hour has come, Polly, may He be strong in you. And, Polly, this burden will be lightened not only by His help but by my presence. It has been decided that, such is the importance of my vocation as a writer, the urgency that I finish my seminal work on Revelations, that I should remain here at present; I will be on hand, to guide and inspire you.' Polly's heart sank; with Drogue around, there was still a long way to go. 'We will discuss your new position tomorrow evening, and announce it to our brothers and sisters. Now, I feel we should pray together.'

Edward was at the evening prayer meeting; she managed not to look at him, though she felt his eyes on her. Afterwards, up in her room, she pulled out the list of Followers she kept tucked inside the pages of her Bible; Bethany, Meg, Bart, Dean, all done for, and the others were in her power – well, soon would be, now that Drogue trusted her. Sandra was still a threat, but all the same, it looked as if Felicity might be right yet again; she was really beginning to see her way to getting Cottenham back.

But Edward – oh, Edward. She lay on the bed and cried heartbrokenly into her pillow.

The news of Polly's elevation didn't seem to surprise the remaining members of the committee when they met next morning under Polly's chairmanship. They seemed almost to have forgotten that she'd once been the mistress of Cottenham; over the past months she'd become simply a reliable figure working around the building in the blue boiler-suit – she'd carefully donned it this morning, no point in going too fast. Only Adrian shifted uneasily in his chair – he would have been the obvious choice as the new Director, Polly realised, and she might have some problems there. She smiled at him sweetly, and he subsided sulkily into his chair. Sandra was notably absent.

Drogue had more or less clarified her duties; chiefly, she'd have far more responsibility for the administration. At last she'd have a chance to get into the files, perhaps trace Jessica . . . Drogue had looked dubiously, disappointedly at the boiler-suit.

'Polly, now that you have been raised to an executive position in God's ranks . . . our Maker frowns on gaudy apparel, but you may feel you wish to clothe yourself more in keeping with your new station. That simple little dress you were wearing last night was most appropriate.' Polly thought it best not to tell him that the simple little dress had cost over two hundred pounds. 'We can manage you an allowance if you need it; now, nothing too expensive, and no low necklines, please! "A modest woman honours the Lord".' He smiled roguishly; clearly he was thinking back to the cream dress she'd worn the night of their first meeting.

'Thank you, Jim, I appreciate your thoughtfulness; my needs are few, our Father will surely supply most of them.' Certainly, any sort of allowance would help, there was no sign of anything more from Edward, in spite of the sale of the company, and the snuffbox money was disappearing fast, mainly on the rent of the flat. She could give the flat up, now that there was a chance of getting Cottenham back – she'd have to go up to town and organise that, clear out her and Muffy's things. How she'd manage for money in the future she didn't know, she'd think of something.

Jim beamed approval when she talked of a visit to London. 'I was going to suggest such a visit to you: as you realise, our numbers have been sadly, unfortunately, depleted, and we shall need to move some of our growing team of members from our other houses to Cottenham. We need young people, Polly, a fresh vision here. We will arrange a series of meetings; I'm trusting you to screen new possibilities for our committee. I, of course, will have the final say.' Polly's spirits rose; she felt certain she could sort out a few trouble-free young things whom it wouldn't be too difficult to shift later.

'Tonight we should hold a special prayer session,' Drogue went on. 'And – one last thing – we have a little problem with Sandra. I don't know if you have any ideas but, as her sister in Christ, I thought I could rely on you to help her to accept her new, humbler role among the Followers.'

Polly smiled modestly, with downcast eyes. 'Actually, Jim, the Lord has spoken to me about Sandra. Do you remember me telling you about our house in France . . .?'

Supper that evening was quite festive: Meredith, on cooking duty, had made a delicious fruit crumble with bottled apricots and pears from the walled garden, and Polly reminded herself to keep her in the kitchen full-time when she finally took over. After the prayer session Simon played his guitar for a while, then Drogue got to his feet.

'More announcements, I'm afraid, though this won't take long.'

First he told them that new members of the committee were to be recruited; Adrian's request that these should be chosen democratically was brushed aside, and he continued: 'Now for a move forward which I think you will find very exciting. All our ideas come from God; I have to tell you that the one I am about to share with you was channelled through Polly here, who is already proving herself the trusty servant we had hoped.

'As you know, the Followers are already active around the world, but there are parts which, sadly, have not yet been touched by God's grace. We are proposing to send a small group to France, to bring His word to those who are in almost total darkness, to draw the lost sheep into the fold . . . Yes?' A hand had shot up; it was one of the new trainees, a blond boy of about eighteen.

'Excuse me, aren't the French already Catholics?' Jim cast him an impatient look.

'Some of them do have their own beliefs, beliefs which are shrouded in darkness and untruth. They need enlightenment, the enlightenment of true faith. Do you realise that many Roman Catholics are not even familiar with the whole Bible, are not allowed to read it?' A gasp went up. 'What hunger, what thirst is there! We shall bring them to the wells of the spirit! We shall show them the light of salvation! And who better to lead this mission than our sister Sandra here?'

*

'So how did she take it?'

Polly was sitting, the next morning, in Toby's kitchen. Muffy, installed for the summer holidays, was out with Toby and the horses, but Harry and Ruth had dropped by just as Polly arrived.

'Amazed – she looked straight at me. Of course, she knew something was up. I just smiled. It all looks very practical, you see; really, she wouldn't want to hang about now I'm in charge, and it's like a nice new job for her. Talking about nice new jobs, Ruth, when are you starting yours?'

After a recovery which had stunned the doctors, Ruth would soon be going back to work on *House in Style*. In fact, she was being promoted; the current editor had resigned, and Ruth had been offered the job. She was still her dear self, but now she radiated confidence and energy; her cheeks were rosy, she'd put on some weight, and a wonderful crop of springy grey curls had replaced her rather sparse mousy hair.

Muffy came in. 'Gosh, Ruth, you look terrific! Any news of Dave? And what's all this about the Followers going to France, Mum? I heard in the village, they can't wait to get rid of the lot of them.'

'Me too,' said Polly, 'but it's only some of them.'

'Where to? Oh no, Mum, not our lovely French house! How many of them are going? Won't they make a mess of it, like they have at Cottenham?'

'They won't be around for long enough,' said Polly. 'You know what the people are like out there.'

It had taken years for Edward and Polly to ingratiate themselves with their more classy French neighbours, longer to get in with the villagers. The curé, Père Martin, had been the last to nod, grudgingly, when he saw them. A cross old man with a deep hatred of foreigners, he ruled his flock with a rod of iron, all the more sternly wielded because of the difficulties of keeping them on the straight and narrow. The modern temptations inveighed against from Catholic pulpits – contraception, abortion – weren't so much the problem; the peasants, deeply conservative, dealt with these as they always had. But the village was in the heart of Cathar country; although, officially, the last pockets of this tenacious belief had been wiped out generations before, it was so deeply ingrained that some of the old ways still survived; Père Martin was, therefore, obsessively concerned with the spiritual beliefs and practices of his people; outside interference of any kind would be not only resented, but dealt with. Polly knew Sandra wouldn't stand a chance; she'd be back home in a month or so, discredited, and that should be the end of her.

'When's she going?' Ruth asked. 'Soon?'

'In a few weeks, I suppose. She'll be taking about six of them, to start with. God knows how old Georgette will take it, and Hector. But they're still being paid, and I suppose we can top it up from Follower funds if they complain.'

'Maybe I'll go out there, a bit later.' Muffy was wearing an artfully casual expression which Polly knew all too well.

'With Sandra? Are you mad? Anyway, you'll have to be back at school in no time.' A suspicion crossed Polly's mind. 'Muffy, you haven't been sacked again?'

There was a muffled snort of laughter from Harry. Muffy sighed. 'Well, Mum – I should have given you the letter before.' She rummaged in her shoulder-bag and found a crumpled envelope, addressed to the London flat. Polly couldn't summon the energy to open it – she knew the contents already.

'Muffy, you are the end. I'm just not going to try again. You'll be seventeen in a month or so, you can get a job like you said you wanted to.'

'But I'm going to be near at hand to help you, Mummy dear.'

And stay on with Toby. Why was the idea so disquieting? 'Well, one thing you can help me with is clearing out the London flat,' Polly said. 'No – ' as Muffy set up a wail of protest ' – I'm afraid there's no help for it, Muffy; we've got to give it up.'

Although Polly stayed on at the farmhouse until nearly lunchtime, Toby did not appear. She wasn't sure if she was glad or sorry.

The seats had to come out of the Followers' bus so that Polly could use it to transport their things from the London flat; on the morning of departure, she took great pleasure in getting Adrian and Simon to do the work, while Meredith and Judy cleared one of the attic rooms, ready to receive her belongings. She did think, briefly, of taking one or other of them with her, to help her load up, but she and Muffy would manage – she'd been surprised by her own strength during the past months of hard work. The rocking-horse was really the heaviest thing, and she had a feeling it could be taken apart. She sent Simon to fetch a screwdriver.

At the last minute, however, Muffy disappeared. Polly waited and waited, but the morning was slipping away; she had to get going. At last she rang the farm, but Toby had no idea where she was.

'You sound worried.' Of course she was worried, after what had happened to Jessica.

'I'm just puzzled – she wanted to come, and I need her, rather, to move the things.' Polly knew how desolate the task would be, all by herself. There was a pause.

'I could come,' Toby said.

The possibility hung in the air between them.

'Thank you, Toby,' she said crisply, 'but I think I'll manage on my own' – and then, when she had put the receiver down, wondered why she couldn't have said yes to him, as she wanted to.

CHAPTER 17

She got to the flat much later than she'd meant to, but the packing went well, and by eight o'clock Polly had more or less finished. The only major thing not packed away was the rocking-horse; after inspecting the way it was put together, she decided she would leave it for the time being – it looked as if it would need a spanner or something, and there might be one in the tool kit in the van. She would deal with it tomorrow. And tomorrow morning she would interview the prospective Followers at Connaught Square – she dreaded seeing the house again – and tomorrow afternoon she would talk to the lawyer, take the keys of the flat back to the agent – and be off.

She decided to have a nice long bath – she was filthy after all that packing – and was just about to turn the hot tap on when the doorbell rang. It was Muffy.

'Muffy! What the hell are you doing here?'

'I thought you wanted me.' Muffy looked hurt. 'So I begged Toby to bring me down. He's parking the landrover, he'll be forever, you know there's never a space round here.'

'I did want you, but I'm all done now. Where were you this morning? I looked everywhere.'

'I was down at Mr Hibbert's,' said Muffy. 'Trudy's had another litter, the puppies are so sweet. Couldn't we have one, to make up for horrible Robert taking Rosie out of our lives?' she wheedled. 'I'm sorry, I just forgot the time.'

The doorbell rang again; it would be Toby.

It was Adrian. Dumb with surprise, Polly led him into the flat.

He looked rather nervously at Muffy – he must have expected Polly to be alone. 'I hope I'm not disturbing you,' he said. 'I thought you might need help.' His rather high-pitched voice had a faint whining note in it. Muffy sat down, interested, on one of the boxes.

Polly gathered her wits; she was on her own ground, she was the mistress now. But did he know about her involvement in Meg's accident, the downfall of Bart, Dean, Bethany? Did he know she was a fraud? Had he come to blackmail her? Or had Drogue sent him to spy on her?

'I expressly said I didn't want anyone to come with me.' Polly made her voice deliberately crisp. 'I'm afraid you must learn to do as I tell you – you must learn the great Christian virtue of obedience.'

'I felt the Lord was guiding me to speak to you,' Adrian responded, flushing; 'felt I should tell you, privately, of the cause of evil in our midst.' He paused for a moment, then burst out: 'And since I've been led hither, I'll reveal it. It's your daughter there, who has led me into temptation – who has put dark and lustful thoughts into my heart, with her wiles. It is she who's spread disruption in our midst.' Muffy was gazing at him with fascination and horror. He'd walked across the room and was standing by the window. 'She must be cast out, for the devil is in her!' Polly was transfixed – she'd never expected this. His voice was rising even higher. 'She must no longer taint our community with her presence. "If there be one among you who offends, cut him off from the body of Christ."'

Muffy had risen to her feet. 'You dirty old thing, how dare you!' she said, and gave him a great push. He lurched sideways in front of the rocking-horse; it swung back and then forward, one of the sharp wooden ears connecting with his skull.

There was a second's silence; Muffy, deathly pale under her freckles, gasped and put her hands over her mouth in the classic gesture of horror. Polly pulled a cushion from the top of one of the bags and lifted up his head to prevent the flow of blood spilling over the carpet. The doorbell rang again; she paused, then hurried to answer it. This time, thank goodness, it was Toby.

His face was arrested in mid-smile; he was looking at the front of her dress, and looking down too, Polly saw that it was streaked with blood.

'Are you all right?' Toby said, taking her arm in a vice-like grip. She nodded without speaking, and he strode past her into the sitting-room, and took in the sight of Adrian on the floor, with Muffy squatting beside him.

Muffy looked up. 'He's alive,' she said in a tremulous voice.

Toby stared down at the body. 'Good God, who is it?' he asked – Toby had always kept as far away from the Followers as he could, and obviously didn't recognize Adrian as one of them. 'How did he get in? Have you rung the police?'

'No,' Polly replied. She'd got to do something, but the police! It would be so difficult to explain, and whatever she said she and Muffy would still be involved, and she couldn't afford that, not now, when she was so near getting Cottenham back, Jessica . . .

'It's too complicated – we've got to get him out of here and to a hospital or something, quickly.'

She knelt down, tying a towel from the bathroom round Adrian's head. 'At least the bleeding's stopped,' said Muffy. She was still pale, but she'd recovered her composure.

Toby, bless him, made no argument but simply got on with the job. They managed between them to shroud Adrian, still mercifully unconscious, in a bedcover and get him into the landrover; Polly had carried a number of bundles and boxes out of the flat that afternoon, the neighbours were hardly going to notice one more.

'Where shall we take him?' Toby asked.

'Royal Free's the nearest,' Muffy said. 'You know the way, Mum, you had to take me there when I cut my foot. We'll have to just slip him in there without them seeing us.' Toby looked doubtful, but Polly remembered the casualty department of the huge Hampstead hospital well; the over-worked staff would hardly notice an unannounced arrival.

'Won't the landrover be a bit conspicuous?'

Muffy gave Toby a pitying look: 'Toby dear, every respectable London mummy has one to drive the kids to school. Let's go.'

They were lucky; no one was about at the entrance, and just inside the door they found a wheelchair.

They thought of leaving him in the corridor, but he was showing signs of consciousness, and he needed attention. Toby, with his striking height and country tweeds, Polly with her looks and her blood-stained dress, would be noticed; Muffy, in her tattered skirt, tennis shoes and rugger shirt, would pass for normal in this part of the world. She wheeled him through, and returned in seconds, triumphant.

The following day Polly completed her business in London and then returned to Cottenham. All the time, in spite of Muffy's reassurances, she worried ceaselessly about Adrian; she was certain he'd come back and tell Drogue what had happened.

'He'll never spill the beans, Mum. And if he does, I'll tell them he molested me – technically I'm a minor, you know.'

'Yes – I almost wish we'd kept him there, and got the police. It would look so sinister, that we smuggled him out of the flat . . . Just as well you're so calm about it.'

Muffy smiled, rather smugly. 'I'll sort it out, Mum.'

And that evening Polly heard from the police that Adrian had been found; she was able to announce to the Followers at the evening prayer meeting that, according to the police, he'd been mugged in one of the side-roads near the Royal Free Hospital and brought in by a passing stranger. 'Truly the act of a Good Samaritan,' Polly said with the new, sweet smile she was practising. 'Our prayers have been answered, and soon our brother Adrian will be with us again.'

She dreaded his reappearance, of course, but when he arrived back two days later, his head still bandaged, his manner hangdog, he seemed newly biddable – though Muffy kept well away. Among the Followers, she made much of the evils his mysterious, unauthorised trip to London had brought upon him.

*

The next couple of weeks passed uneventfully; the recruits she had picked in London with such care – she knew they'd have to pass muster with Jim Drogue – settled in. As she had intended, they couldn't be faulted on the grounds of their faith or their Christian zeal, but they all lacked any of the disturbing individuality or initiative which could have made them potentially dangerous to her position.

Drogue, busy with his book, left her more and more in charge of the day-to-day administration of Cottenham, which she found tedious, but less difficult than she'd feared. She found she had a talent for delegation; Adrian ran the courses, Muffy checked the accounts for her. There was masses of paperwork – faxes from the States, Connaught Square, the other Follower branches, flowed in; Simon dealt with those, under her supervision. She'd got quite fond of him – so much so that when a friend sent her the Sotheby's catalogue featuring the red-robed cardinals from Connaught Square with a note: 'I always admired these – what a shame you didn't give me first chance to make an offer,' she simply called Simon in and told him to get the pictures back, fast.

With all this help, with Judy looking after the house, and delicious meals coming up from the kitchen under Meredith's supervision, she was almost at the point where she could begin to change Cottenham back to what it had been, though she still felt she couldn't be truly comfortable until Sandra was gone. And until Jessica was back.

Edward, she knew, had gone – he was back in Russia. At least his geographical distance meant she didn't think of him so much. Often, she thought about Toby. That ghastly evening in London seemed to have overcome their embarrassment with each other; she'd been so grateful for the unquestioning practicality with which he'd helped to shift Adrian – she couldn't help comparing it with the way Edward might have behaved. There was an open warmth, a gentleness between them now that gave her great comfort.

Late one afternoon, she was working at her desk – she'd moved into her own bedroom, which doubled as an office – when the phone rang, and she picked it up to hear an unmistakable voice say:

'Polly? It's Felicity. I've heard from Jessica.'

Polly's heart lurched, first with joy and relief, then with hurt. Why hadn't Jess contacted her? The questions tumbled out: 'Is she all right? Where is she? Is she coming back?'

'The letter was posted in London; she's in the States, she didn't say where. She's all right. Look, I'll read it to you.'

The message was brief, but Jessica had always found writing difficult.

'Oh, Felicity – thank God – if only we knew where she was.'

A great wave of longing to see her, touch her, overcame Polly. She pulled herself together. 'Felicity, thank you so much for ringing – please let me know if you hear any more.' She must go over to the farm and tell Muffy.

Muffy was overjoyed by the news – Toby opened a bottle of wine to celebrate, and they spent a convivial evening together.

'If only I wasn't off to France,' Muffy said, 'I could get out to the States and do some sleuthing – I'll come straight back if she turns up . . .'

Polly had almost forgotten that she would soon be going with Sandra. Muffy had begged and wheedled so importunately – 'I'd be as good as gold with the Followers, Mum; I could keep an eye on the house, and just think how good it would be for my French!' – that at last Polly had given in. She'd miss her; and she also felt a strange sense of foreboding.

'You'll take care, won't you, darling?' she asked anxiously. Muffy, practically buried under Toby's springer spaniel, glanced across at her:

'I can look after myself.'

Apart from her stay in Geneva, Sandra had hardly been out of England before, and she'd never visited the château – they'd bought it after Muffy had ceased to need a full-time nanny, and they'd always had Georgette there to organise things. Her spirits had risen visibly as the day for departure drew nearer; among other things, she'd been busy putting together her clothes for the trip, a wardrobe suitable for a Mediterranean holiday. Polly was treated to a preview when she called Sandra in for a final briefing; sundresses in vibrant tropical colours suspended on shoestring straps over Sandra's thickening shoulders, T-shirts that looked dangerously tight for Sandra's solid bust. Polly wondered how well they would go down; the wives of the local gentry, in true French style, made few concessions to the weather, changing their tweed skirts to flannel, their cashmere sweaters to a shirt; older villagers might swap their winter black for a modest print. Polly began to feel a slight unease at the trap she had set for Sandra. She leant forward.

'Are you prepared, fully prepared?' she asked solemnly. Sandra simpered.

'We who serve the Lord are always prepared, as you now know, Polly. This is a great commission which has been set on me, and I shall look to His strength in me for success. I have just been with Jim – Mr Drogue – who has given me a final blessing.'

High time she went then, Polly thought, quelling all her previous doubts. She gave Sandra the keys of the house, some last minute notes, and added her own blessing for good measure.

The minibus drew away the next morning for the start of the long trip south, Muffy waving wildly out of a back window. Polly went inside; with Sandra gone, she could start to reverse the horrors the Followers had perpetrated at Cottenham. There was still enough of the snuffbox money to make a start; she'd got cheap labour on the spot, and Drogue was so fully occupied with his book, he'd hardly notice. It would be easier if he wasn't there, of course.

Muffy rang a few days later – everything was going fine, lovely weather – and at the end of the week Sandra's written report arrived. Much good work was in hand; they'd already drawn up a plan for visits among the local people, for an extended mission in the nearby schools; the sample material they'd taken seemed to be meeting with a warm reception. Some difficulties in contacting the local minister. She ended with a patronising appraisal of the house, and signed off with the usual praise and blessings.

Polly breathed a sigh of relief – her premonitions of real trouble were clearly unfounded, Sandra would just come up against a blank wall with the villagers, the curé, and come back disheartened, discredited. It would be the end of her.

CHAPTER 18

The next few days passed peacefully. The only surprise was that, among a new group of Followers to come and stay at Cottenham, there was a familiar face: Steve, from the Centre.

'Hi, Polly,' he said, grinning, when it was his turn to come up and shake her hand at the formal welcoming of the new recruits.

'Oh, Steve. Hallo.' Could it really be him? She'd never have imagined he would stay the course – he hadn't seemed to fit in at the Centre at all.

With some supervision, Polly's team were well able to organise the lectures and workshops the new group needed, so she had time on her hands. She hired a couple of pneumatic drills and had them out each afternoon, taking up the tarmac over the rose beds. The extension the Followers had built at the back of the house would have to stay, for the moment – it was quite well placed. She toyed with the idea of glassing it in and making a giant conservatory.

Then came Muffy's next phone call. It was less reassuring than the last one.

'It's not so good, Mum, the villagers are up in arms, a group of them came here yesterday to speak to Sandra. And Georgette and Hector won't come up to the château any more, I think Père Martin's forbidden them to.'

Polly cursed herself for her folly – suppose things got really out of hand? They'd have to come back. 'Get me Sandra on the phone,' she barked. She stood, picking at her nails, while down the telephone she could hear shouts resounding through the hall of the château. Finally she heard the sound of feet on the stone floor, and Sandra's voice.

'I gather you're somewhat disturbed, Polly, but I assure you all is well. We have, of course, encountered a little opposition, but surely we expected this – we must suffer for our faith. There are those here, I can tell, who are ready in their hearts to come to Christ . . .'

Polly realised now, with full force, what a misjudgment she'd made; the new, humble Sandra, briefly glimpsed, was only a mask. She was relishing her powers, she wouldn't relinquish them for anything. Summoning all her authority, Polly said: 'You are to return, Sandra, all of you.'

'God's calling cannot be denied – we must do His bidding.'

The line went dead – Polly stared at the receiver. Had Sandra cut her off deliberately? But when she rang again, and again, there was no reply.

Clearly, Sandra wasn't going to budge. Polly cast around in her mind for what to do. Drogue could be a useful ally, though it wounded her pride to have to ask for his help. She pushed open the door of his study.

'Ah, Polly, you have come at a God-given moment – I would like to read you the penultimate paragraphs of my fifth section. There will be two more, to mirror the incidences of this number in the text. I've always felt, as you know, that Revelations, well-trodden territory though it is, has been misunderstood. Here, as I think you'll realise, I have been enabled to throw new light . . .'

'I'll come back later,' said Polly. It would take too long to bring him down to earth. Toby! She'd talk to Toby – why hadn't she thought of him before? She changed her shoes in the hall, and ran across the fields.

'We'll have to get out there,' he said, after she'd told him about the phone call.

'Oh, Toby, would you come?' she gasped.

'Of course – it may be tricky. We'll try the airlines, pick up a car the other end . . .' He was already on the phone.

Everything was booked until late the next afternoon, they'd have to change planes in Paris. At least it gave Polly time to hand things over to Adrian for a few days; she simply told him she was going out to check up on things in France.

The flights went smoothly enough, it was only as they neared the house that Polly became overcome by panic. What if anything had happened to Muffy? And she'd only wanted Sandra humiliated, not actually harmed. It was past midnight. She guided Toby up the back way; they swept along the leafy avenue in the little rented Peugeot. Round at the front, the porch light shone under the great carved coat-of-arms; by its light, she could see that the bushes were trampled, two panes of glass were broken. The door was open. Clutching Toby's arm, she went inside.

Apart from the glass, and a few small stones on the floor, there was no further damage. People had been in the house recently; an open book lay on a table, *Sharing our Faith Journey* – Toby looked at it and snorted – there was a burnt-out fire in the hearth, but nobody was about. Together they looked through the lower rooms, then climbed, Polly with a beating heart, to Muffy's little tower room. Here, her clothes were spread about, clearly recognisable in their disorder. Polly looked around for a note, a clue as to where she might be – nothing. She raced downstairs and outside, and almost fell into the arms of Hector, who appeared to be searching the bushes with a torch.

'Where are they all? Where's Muffy?'

'Gone, all gone.' Hector was a man of few words. Then: 'Your daughter's at our place.' Surprising herself, Polly kissed him on both cheeks, and ran to the car, Toby just a few paces behind her.

It took only a couple of minutes to reach Georgette and Hector's cottage. Georgette, in a pastel floral wrapper, opened the door. Her eyes narrowed at the sight of Toby, but when Polly reminded her who he was, she shook hands, then broke into a stream of incomprehensible, rapid French and went to make coffee. Polly only caught a few phrases, many of them none too complimentary: 'filthy pigs', 'pagans', 'English unbelievers'. Then, to Polly's utter relief and delight, Muffy came sleepily through from the best front room. Speech was impossible against the vigorous flow of Georgette's French – Muffy kissed Toby and clung to her mother. At last, still talking, Georgette went to bed, making doom-laden gestures with her hands as she mounted the stairs.

'So what happened?' Polly asked, now that they could talk. The three of them sat down on Georgette's battered old sofa.

'Things were bad already,' said Muffy – for the moment, she seemed quite calm – 'so I could see there was going to be trouble today. It's their big annual festival, the villagers, they were going to have a special mass in the morning, and then this terrific party in the square in the evening.'

'So?' Hector had come in. He delved in a dark cupboard and produced a bottle of cognac which he put on the table. Muffy was shivering violently now. Toby poured her a glassful – she drank, coughed and went on:

'Sandra was waiting outside the church after mass, in that sundress, you know, with a load of leaflets. All the others had banners. None of the villagers took much notice of them then, they all went home to lunch – but the Followers came back in the evening, when the *fête* started.'

Hector took up the story; his French, slower and sparser, was a whole lot more comprehensible than Georgette's:

'Some of the boys got a bit drunk; they started to laugh at the English people. Père Martin had spoken about them in his sermon – he said they were mocking our beliefs. Then the English woman stood on a box and started to give a talk – nobody liked it much, we wanted to enjoy the *fête* – and the English people sang, and gave out leaflets; I must say, at first they were quite brave. But after a bit one or two of the younger ones ran away, and some of our boys took the English woman off into the wood. She was making a lot of noise.'

Polly and Toby exchanged horrified glances. 'I think the boys went up to your place after that,' Hector went on, 'they were saying these missionary people shouldn't be there. I don't know what they did, but in the end the English left, in their bus. Of course, I went up to the château myself,' he added self-righteously, 'as soon as I could, but I was running the raffle, you see. Monsieur Legrand, the old chap, won the pig this year.'

They sat in stunned silence while he poured them all another cognac. 'Georgette brought your daughter down here,' he said, 'we didn't want her in any trouble.'

Polly pulled herself together. 'So did the Englishwoman go in the bus?'

'No, they found her in the woods – she's all right. She's at the priest's house.'

Hector stood up; he obviously felt there was nothing more to be said. 'Well, there's work to do tomorrow. The girl had better stay here for the night.'

Polly and Toby made their way back to the house. The big double room hadn't been used; there seemed to be no point in bustling around changing the other beds. They fell into it and, worn out, rather drunk, fell fast asleep.

Polly was tense with a variety of fears as she approached the presbytery next morning. She still had no clear idea of the state Sandra was in, whether she'd seen a doctor – the villagers might well not have called one, just to keep the matter hushed up. Then, though she and Edward were now on reasonable terms with Père Martin (a large donation to the church funds had helped), she'd always been scared of him; somehow he reminded her too much of a fierce visiting confessor she'd had at school. And although it was early, he might well have heard that she'd spent the night alone with her brother-in-law up at the château; all the gossip reached him through the team of devout village women who cleaned his house. One of these opened the door to her and Muffy – she'd thought it best to leave Toby behind.

Père Martin was out, it seemed, and they were shown straight up to the first floor.

Polly had expected almost anything except what she saw. Sandra was sitting up in state in the sagging brass bed that occupied the presbytery's spare bedroom, her cheeks slightly flushed, her hands folded calmly on the front of a borrowed winceyette nightdress, a faint smile on her face. Mme Legrand, who'd sometimes come up to help at the château, was fussing around her.

'Sandra – are you all right? We're here to take you back to England.' They'd decided that, however unwelcome her company might be, there was nothing else for it.

Sandra motioned Polly to a chair with a queenly gesture. 'I'm being well looked after, as you can see.' She nodded graciously towards Mme Legrand. 'But I don't think I shall be well enough to travel for some time.' She lowered her voice. 'Terribly bruised – I didn't realise that poor boy felt so passionately about me, though I had suspected there was an attraction there. But then, these young men . . .' she sighed reminiscently '. . . we have to understand, and forgive. It's a pity he was less susceptible to the Gospel. However, our work may yet bear fruit . . .'

Polly and Muffy were speechless as they descended the long chestnut treads of Père Martin's beautiful staircase. In the hall, Père Martin himself was waiting.

'Ah, you have had a word with this poor misguided woman.'

To Polly's astonishment, the curé's crusty old face was soft with – what was it? Sympathy? Admiration even? It looked almost as if Sandra's experience had transformed her, in his eyes, into some kind of saint or martyr, no matter what her beliefs. 'Don't worry,' he went on, 'we will look after her, her body will heal, it is her spirit I fear for. But we will work on her, there is a flicker of faith there, all is not lost.'

Polly couldn't believe it; he was smiling, obviously delighted at the thought of the task ahead.

'So you think she didn't mind about it?' Toby asked.

'I don't think she realised it was rape; she honestly thought the boy was overcome with passion for her,' Polly said. 'Does it count as rape if you don't think it is? I mean, she must have had some idea of what was going on. But the amazing thing was Père Martin taking her in like that. I've never seen him look so cheerful. Perhaps he'll keep her on as his housekeeper, then they could spend the rest of their days converting each other!'

They were sitting with their drinks on the terrace of a hotel high above the Dronne. Georgette and Hector, generously tipped, had tidied up the château, and Polly had been anxious to get back to Cottenham as soon as possible, but it was Muffy's birthday, and she'd begged for a night to recover from it all. She was standing further down the terrace; Toby had bought her a ridiculous hat in a local shop; wearing it, she was pitching small stones far down into the river.

So Sandra was settled, Polly thought, possibly for good. The scared party of young Followers had set off north in the minibus, apparently to an evangelical centre in Rouen; they could look after themselves. She'd have to think of a way of clearing the rest of them out of Cottenham, then it would finally be in her hands again. Could she actually begin to tell herself now that she'd won – against all the odds, and out of her own sheer tenacity and refusal to give in? Beautiful, feckless Polly; had she proved herself something more than that, as Felicity believed she could?

Polly took a sip of her gin and stared out over the river. Too early yet for self-congratulation; Cottenham and Connaught Square still belonged to the Followers, and most important of all, Jessica was still absent. If only she would come back . . . And if only, Polly thought, I knew who was behind the whole Followers thing; if only I knew who was the top man. She still hadn't found out, after all this time. Somehow, until she knew, she wouldn't be able to feel really safe.

She shivered slightly; the sun was setting and the cooler air was rising from the river. Toby put an arm round her shoulders, and they went in to dinner.

She and Muffy dropped Toby off at the entrance to the farm – he was anxious about the horses – and went on to Cottenham together. It felt as if a year had passed since they had left, not just three days, Polly thought as they drove up to the front entrance, but little had changed; the remaining Followers had taken up a few more metres of the well-laid tarmac, the trees had that tired, end-of-summer look. That car parked by the door – surely that could only be Felicity's ancient Bentley?

Even as she was wondering, a large and beautiful young man came down the steps with a girl. Jessica!

Polly skidded to a stop on the gravel, ran blindly to meet her. As she flung her arms round her, she came up against the hard bump of her abdomen; Jessica was pregnant. Crying and laughing with joy, Polly kissed and kissed her, pushed the hair away from her face and kissed her again, Muffy fighting for space beside her. The young man watched quietly as the three women embraced.

'But you're safe – where were you? We've been so worried! Are you all right? And a baby!' Polly patted the bulge, couldn't resist looking enquiringly round at the young man as he leant against the porch.

Jessica moved back a little. 'I've been fine; I met Jake at La Guardia. I was getting a bit fed up with the Followers – would you believe it, they were thinking of a new name for me, Martha they came up with! So we just sort of moved off together. We've been in this commune in New Mexico, it was great. Didn't Edward tell you where I'd gone, or Jim?'

Polly thought she had never before heard Jessica say so much in one go. But one particular thing she had said hit her like a blow. 'So Edward did know where you were?' Any last feeling she had had for him died in that moment.

'Yes, and Jim – I felt bad I'd given him the slip, but, well, you know how it is.' She put her arm around Jake's waist – he beamed down at her. Maybe that was why Jim had been sent to Cottenham – he'd been demoted, he was in disgrace for letting his charge disappear. But she'd think about it all later, Polly told herself; Jessica was back, that was what mattered.

'Felicity's around somewhere,' said Jessica, 'she came to get us.'

'At the airport?' Polly asked.

'No, she flew out, when she'd found out where we were.' She smiled happily, and turned as Felicity herself came down the steps.

'Oh Felicity, thank you, thank you. I'm so sorry I wasn't here when you arrived with her.'

'That's all right,' Felicity said equably, 'Jim Drogue let me in. What a sad little man. I overestimated your opposition, Polly; it can't have taken much to knock him off his perch.'

Polly drew in an outraged breath – but then gritted her teeth on it and said only: 'If you'd told me you'd found her, I would have come out to the States with you . . .'

'It was only a hunch, Polly dear; you see, I have a mass of contacts, and I was trading in one of Tristram's sculptures with a dealer in New York who happened to know some of the people in the commune.' She smiled. 'I sold another one to raise the fare.'

Not for the first time, Polly gazed at her mother-in-law – still wearing what was undoubtedly her driving hat, a curious felt creation battened down and fastened under her chin with a gauzy scarf – and thought that as long as she lived, Felicity would never cease to astonish her.

Muffy danced down the steps. 'Letters, Mum – look, we've got one each of these, nice stamps . . . Mum, what on earth is it?'

They were holding identical cards; the man in the indistinct photograph was certainly Edward, you could not mistake him, but the snowy beard? – Edward hated beards – the hat?

Polly was too bewildered, at first, to feel any emotion. On the back, there was what looked like a religious text in Russian; a tiny handwritten note read: 'I have joined the Russian Orthodox Church, and am training for the priesthood. God bless you. Edward.'

Polly stared at the words for a long time, the others standing silent around her. Somehow, in spite of everything, she already felt this was a blessing she could accept.

They ate in the parlour. By tacit agreement, Muffy and Polly didn't mention Edward and his news, but bombarded Jessica with questions; it was amazing, to be able to ask Jess a question and get an answer back every time, and there was a new, calm quality about her. Jake talked too. The commune, which Polly had pictured as a collection of squalid huts somewhere in the desert, turned out to have been a tasteful arrangement of adobe cottages peopled by well-heeled dropouts in search of their creative selves. The baby was due in five months.

'You'd better stay here,' Polly said to them, 'there's enough room, now.' The diminished Followers had retired to the back of the house, in Adrian's charge. Polly had excused herself from the evening prayer session; she could hear wafts of their lusty singing now. She poured them all another glass of Edward's wine.

When the lovers were settled in Jessica's old room, and Felicity, who insisted on driving home through the night, had been seen off into the summer darkness, Polly went down to talk to Muffy.

'Did you notice, she didn't say a word about Robert?' asked Muffy. 'We'll have to tell her some time.'

'I suppose so. She is a funny girl. Honestly, the agony we've been through – but I'm so happy to have her back, and she's so much better, isn't she? Look, I got a letter from Edward's solicitor in the same post as those cards. Apparently, now he's a priest he wants to live simply and give everything away. Nothing's sorted out yet about money, it's complicated, but he wants me to have the lease on Connaught Square, and Cottenham goes to you, with me there for my life. That's when the Follower leases are up, but it looks as if they're pushing off anyway. And we're to share the château. Toby gets the farms.'

'That's nice, Mum – it's as if he forgave us, minds about us still.' Muffy was tearful. 'But I still don't understand why he did it.'

'I think I had a feeling he'd do something like this,' said Polly slowly. 'It's as if the Followers was a stepping-stone, or he took a wrong turning; he was looking for something, and now he's found it. I hope so, anyway. Don't be sad, Muffy, you could go and see him when we find out where he is. After all, you're a quarter Russian.'

Muffy brightened up a little. Polly hurried on, to distract her: 'I don't want to tell Jessica too much about Edward and the houses and so on at the moment, because we always expected he'd do something for her, didn't we? So it might be a bit hurtful, until we know for sure whether he has.'

'Don't worry, Mum, Jake's loaded – didn't you gather who his family are?' She named a famous Californian tribe. 'Jess will be all right.'

'And how about you, my darling?' She must get something organised for Muffy, Polly thought – after all, the girl was seventeen, she should be occupied, at least, and with Muffy's brains . . . 'Wouldn't you like to train for something?' she asked hopefully.

'Don't you worry about me, Mum, I've got my plans.' She grinned, and said casually, 'By the way, nice to see Steve here, isn't it?'

'I didn't know you knew Steve, Muffy.'

'He was one of the clearance men at Connaught Square, Mum, don't you remember?' That was it, the grin and the tattoos – that's why he had seemed familiar at the Centre. 'When he brought our stuff round to the flat, we found we rather hit it off. Of course, he isn't really a clearance man, Mum,' Muffy went on cheerfully, 'he's an undercover policeman, but you'd better keep that under your hat for the time being.'

CHAPTER 19

Polly had already resolved to sell Connaught Square; she could live on the money realised by the sale, whatever else Edward might give her, and live at Cottenham – though she supposed she'd have to move out if Muffy ever wanted it back. There was still the matter of the leases to the Followers to sort out, but apparently Griersons now thought these could be broken. She'd have to go to London to talk to them about it. She could visit Connaught Square at the same time. She dreaded it, all those alarming people in their expensive suits, but she needed to find out what was going on. The stream of accustomed faxes from London, from the States, seemed to be drying up; the machine was often silent for a day at a time, now. What was happening?

She'd get down there. Meanwhile, the early autumn weather was mild and beautiful; the Followers worked on in the garden, which was beginning to look as if it might, one day, be pretty again – though never the same. Drogue had installed himself in the old wooden summerhouse, where he was still busy on his masterwork; he'd surface, preoccupied, for meals, and Polly had noticed the girls running across with cups of coffee.

'Why do you do it for him, nasty old thing?' she'd asked them.

'He's not, Mum,' Muffy had said, 'he's much better now, and we're sorry for him – Charlene ran off with a golf pro, you know.'

Toby would often come over; she wasn't shy with him any more, they'd chat for hours. They hadn't yet made love, but the knowledge that love was there, waiting for them when they were ready, hung gently in the air between them. Muffy disappeared for much of the time. Jessica lay, smiling beatifically, on a long chair in the garden. Jake, for all his laid-back looks, had shown surprising energy; he was ripping out the attic partitions with his own hands.

'I've fallen in love with this place,' he said to Polly as, disturbingly handsome, dishevelled, he sat down with her under the remaining beech tree. 'I can just picture it, restored to its original state. It certainly needs some money spending on it.'

True, it did need tidying; what was left of the furniture was all over the place, they'd never even got the things from the London flat out of the hall and up into the attics. All the same, Jake's words made Polly feel rather cross; what did he envisage, beyond taking it back to what it had been before the Followers moved in? *She* was the one who was in love with Cottenham, and she hadn't fought to get it back for Jake to do it up. Anyway, it belonged to Muffy, or would do, when she had sorted things out with Griersons. She'd go to London tomorrow, and hurry back; Ruth had rung, she wanted to come over for the night and talk. She'd sounded strange – Polly hoped to God the cancer hadn't come back again.

She spent an hour and a half with Mr Grierson; yes, the money realised by the sale of Edward's worldly assets would come through within a few months; if there was any hold-up, it would be because there seemed to be some odd discrepancies in the amounts which had been paid into various trusts. There wouldn't be a vast amount for Polly and the girls: Edward was using most of it to set up a factory (pencils), build a school and a hospital to help the people near Saratov, where he was settling. The transfer of the deeds to the houses would be quicker. Mr Grierson confirmed that the leases to the Followers wouldn't be too difficult to break, he'd already had a good look at them, and would get to work on the matter straightaway. Eyeing Polly, sun-tanned, long-haired again, long-legged in her blue-checked linen suit, he asked whether she wouldn't like to discuss the details over lunch? But she was too anxious to get the visit to Connaught Square over; disappointed, he saw her into a taxi. In twenty minutes she was at the door.

She let herself in with her keys; she felt it was already her house again. In the dining-room, the gilt chairs still stood around her own mahogany table. The sitting-room was empty; the whole place had a hollow feeling. She suddenly felt fearful; she was tempted to call out. As she stood there, uncertainly, she heard footsteps on the staircase.

For a moment she didn't recognise him behind the dark glasses, then she realised who it was. There had always been something about him; something odd, something different. Some uneasy combination of helplessness and ruthlessness that made this ordinary, brown-haired, rather short young man remarkable – and dangerous.

'Dave! What are you doing here?'

For a moment he looked as surprised as she was, then he regained his composure. He took off the dark glasses, carefully put down the black plastic sack he was carrying, kissed her on the cheek as he always had. She recognised his aftershave – where had she smelt it, not so long ago?

'Polly! How lovely to see you. Muffy asked me to pick up some gear for her.'

Muffy? In the old days she'd always had her secrets with Dave, but she hadn't seen him for so long. And surely all her things had been moved to Cottenham some time ago?

Polly's mind raced; she remembered Ruth's worries about Dave, the shifty look he'd had on his face when he was last in England, the perfect clothes. He was stealing! If the bag had been marked 'swag', it couldn't be clearer. Polly moved as fast as her tight skirt would allow – she reached across and ripped. Shredded paper – she started to pull it out in great handfuls.

'Polly, don't do that.'

But it was too late – paper spewed forth: coloured paper, white paper, the green and pink of cheques, thick and thin, handwritten, printed, their content lost and jumbled but a word, a figure decipherable here and there. There was nothing else.

Everything suddenly fell into place.

'So, you were behind the Followers? You were their leader?'

A terrible anger overcame Polly. Edward, the houses, Jessica's disappearance, the dreadful things she'd done – had all been his fault. All the effort, the weariness; the hard new person she'd become; it was all because of this ridiculous boy.

She moved towards him, then stopped. If he was shredding documents, it must mean someone was already after him. She sank down on the bottom stair, exhausted. Dave was smiling – she remembered that smile from when he'd been little.

'Why did you do it?' she said. She already knew the answer. 'Was it for the money?'

'Yes. It was so easy.' Again, the smile. 'I just had to put up a good front, and it came rolling in. There was this huge funding from the States, you see, and then they were all lined up over here, just waiting to hand it out. And I liked it.' He sat down on the stair beside her. 'I went places I'd never have got to otherwise – and the power, bossing those idiots around. They got out of hand, though, like you were going to.'

'You mean,' Polly said slowly, 'you arranged for me to get into the Followers?' She'd always puzzled over the way that had happened.

'Yes,' he answered simply. 'Drogue was always a bit above himself, you see, and the whole English thing was getting too independent. I didn't want it that way – and I knew you'd put paid to it. And you did, more or less!' He smiled once more. 'I suppose I had it in for Drogue. And that fiasco with Mum was one more black mark.'

'You knew about that? How could you have let them do it? And did you feel anything for their beliefs, these people?'

Dave looked puzzled. 'Why, no.'

Polly stared at him; how hard it was to make the leap into someone else's mind. He clearly, unimaginably, had no regrets. It was indeed like dealing with a child. She must ask him one more thing.

'Why on earth did you think I could sort the Followers out?'

'You're a strong woman, Polly, I've always known it, under that helpless exterior. And a very attractive one. You haven't lost anything on it, by the way, or just ask our friend Drogue if you find you have.' Hadn't lost anything? Only a husband, a whole way of life. 'Now, dear honorary godmother, you're not going to tell on me, are you? I'm in a bit of trouble already, or will be unless I move fast. And think what it would do to Ruth.'

He bent to kiss her; then, leaving her among the debris of paper fragments, he crossed to the door and was gone.

No, Ruth mustn't know. And there was her own involvement, which he'd so carefully arranged; she had her secrets, now. Anyway, what was to be gained by telling? The 'important people' whose money had supported the Followers, and Dave, wouldn't want either a scandal or to admit that they'd been duped; and as for herself, she had Jessica back, and Cottenham. One day she might have to tell somebody, but not yet.

Cottenham, as she opened the door, seemed almost as empty as the London house – there was no one in the hall, no sound from the kitchen. Perhaps the Followers had gone on an impromptu outing – sometimes the Lord dictated they should do just that. She'd spotted Jake planting saplings down the garden – they'd decided to replace the lost specimen trees with a little wood – she'd ask him.

He raised a hand as she approached, and loped towards her. 'They've gone,' he called from a few yards off.

'What? Who?'

'The Followers – they've left.' Polly looked across the drive; the second minibus was missing. The Followers seemed to get through minibuses rather fast. 'Adrian came to me, very straight-faced,' Jake went on. 'Apparently he'd called a meeting, he said they were "increasingly disturbed" by the fornication within the walls – he meant Jessica and me, of course. He threw chunks of the Bible at me, then said that unless we regularised our union, we'd have to go. I'm afraid I flipped; I said we'd do what we wanted to do, and in our own good time. Then Muffy joined in and told them the place was hers anyway, and then they packed and went.' He looked at Polly dubiously. 'I'm sorry.'

'Don't worry, I wanted them out. How are the others? How's Jess?'

'Fine. Look, I wanted to talk to you. I've had a word with Muffy; she says she's happy to sell me Cottenham, but that I must ask you. I know you're fond of the old place, there'd be no question of turning you out, we could all live here together . . .'

Fond of the old place indeed! She'd murdered to keep it – well, almost. Yet she could imagine Jake and Jessica living here. She patted his cheek.

'We'll talk, later. I'm worn out.'

Muffy was lying in wait for her in the hall. 'Mum, you wouldn't mind about Cottenham? We could all live here, you know.'

'Darling, it's yours to sell, but don't you want to keep it? Where will you live, when you want a house of your own?'

Muffy shot her a sly look: 'I've been meaning to tell you, Mum – the thing is, I might move in with Steve.'

'Steve – you mean the policeman? So that's what you've been up to all this time!'

'Yes – he's got the dearest little police house, like a dolly's house, I love it, and we could keep a cottage here . . . I asked him over for supper tonight. Toby's coming, and Ruth's here, so I thought you wouldn't mind one extra.'

'Of course not.' Who would cook, with Meredith gone? She realised she might rather miss the Followers. 'Ruth's here already? How lovely. Where is she?'

'She's on the veranda, resting – she said she felt a bit tired.'

Oh, and she'd been so fit, so energetic, after the operation. Polly felt she could hardly bear it. She walked slowly through the passage to where Ruth lay, a rug draped over her.

'Oh, Ruth, Ruth . . .'

Unable to speak, Polly silently took her hand. When she could bear to raise her eyes, she was amazed. Ruth looked marvellous, but it was her expression; mischievous, embarrassed.

'It's all right, it's not what you think, I didn't mean to scare you – Polly, I'm having a baby.'

A baby! Ruth must be forty-four – and the doctors had always said she couldn't have another one. She'd been near death a few months ago, she'd had all sorts of bits and pieces taken out . . .

Ruth laughed out loud at Polly's astonishment. 'I know, I know, it's crazy, but it's true. The doctors say it's a miracle.'

They both looked up as a black-clad figure crossed the lawn from the summerhouse. It was Jim Drogue.

'Polly,' Ruth said, 'you're thinking what I'm thinking, aren't you?'

Their eyes met. 'Yes.'

When the others arrived – Harry and Toby came over, Steve appeared as if from nowhere – they opened a couple of bottles of champagne to celebrate. Before Polly could stop her, Muffy had dragged Drogue away from his book to join in.

'You are tactless, Muffy,' Polly hissed at her, 'with all the other Followers gone.'

'But that's just it, he's lonely. Jess and I have been trying to cheer him up. At least he doesn't come out with that Christian stuff all the time now. He's even thinking of giving up writing that dreary book, poor old thing.'

Poor old thing, indeed. Luckily he didn't recognise the new Ruth – how should he?

Jake cooked them all delicious spaghetti for supper; Ruth took the place of honour, glowing.

'But Ruth, your lovely job – you'll have to give it up!' Jessica said.

'No, Jess, it's all right, they have to bend over backwards for pregnant ladies now; and when she's born, Harry can look after her.' Harry, delighted, had decided it was going to be a girl.

'Hope she'll survive all that plaster dust!' said Muffy. 'Does Dave know he's in for a little sister yet?' Polly's heart lurched.

'We've written,' Ruth said tranquilly; the new pregnancy had already distanced her from her errant son.

They took their coffee through into the drawing-room. It looked rather odd; there were ziggurats of metal chairs around the walls, spotlights on stands, scaffolding for a prefabricated platform stacked in a corner. The now familiar bright Christian posters were pinned up on the panelling; among them Muffy had defiantly hung the Connaught Square pictures Simon had retrieved from Sotheby's. Jake was into early American furniture in a big way, and had already bought several fine pieces for the house – rather prematurely, Polly thought, but she had to admit that their lovely, simple lines suited Cottenham much better than the Lonsdale things. Only a few of these seemed to have survived – the huge, threatening *bergère* sofa she was sitting on with Muffy and Toby was one of them.

'All these babies, Mum – did you know Robert and Alison are expecting, too? Perhaps you and I should join the club.' She laughed raucously at the idea of her mother ever getting pregnant again, and lifted Trudy's puppy onto the sofa with them.

'Muffy, really – as far as I'm concerned, you girls are quite enough trouble.' It had never crossed Polly's mind, but as she turned to Toby she saw him smiling at her speculatively. But what on earth was Muffy suggesting? 'Muffy, if I catch you even thinking of getting pregnant at your age . . . And I'm not at all sure about this idea of moving in with Steve.' She looked across to where Steve was sitting talking to Harry. 'You know I like him, but he won't want you half-educated, hanging about the house.'

'Calm down, Mum, Steve's right on your side, we've got it all mapped out. He wants to talk to you, anyway.'

'It's not Muffy, we can do that some other time,' Steve said. 'It's Jim Drogue.' Polly looked across to Drogue who, livelier for a glass of Edward's brandy, was chatting with Jake; he'd really become almost normal. 'We've been investigating him for months, of course, and the fraud squad have got enough on him to put him away; he's been diverting Follower funds into his own pocket for months, notably a lot of Edward Lonsdale's cash. I just wanted to find out how you felt about it before they go into action. The thing is, it could take the lid off the whole can of worms, they'd have to pull in all the people involved.' He looked across at Ruth.

So he knew about Dave. 'Where is the money?' Polly asked.

'Here and there – there's a whole lot in a bank based in High Wycombe, of all places. He comes from there.'

'I thought he was from Illinois.' The blueberry-picking expeditions, the big whitewashed kitchen Drogue had described, had all been fantasy. Knowing High Wycombe as she did, Polly thought she could understand.

'Just get the money back,' she said, 'it's mine, and Muffy's. We've got enough, but I don't see why we should be cheated. Can you fix that?'

'A pleasure.' Steve gave the cheeky grin she remembered from the Centre, and went back to put a tattooed arm round Muffy.

They'd all gone. She'd seen Toby on his way – she would join him at the farmhouse later – stopping for a long kiss among the azalea bushes. The scanty leaves of the saplings they'd been planting were rustling nearby; in five years they'd be well-grown.

Back at the house, Jake had locked up for her, the girls had tidied the supper away and jollied Jim up to bed, each taking an arm. He was becoming something of a household pet – but he'd have to go. Apart from anything else, as one of the chief Follower lessees, the lease still held while he was around. But she couldn't, wouldn't just throw him out. She poured herself a glass of brandy and sat back to think. Then she pulled the phone across to the sofa.

She'd known Felicity would still be up, in spite of the time. She explained the problem – no need to mention the money, or the miracle. Felicity seemed surprised, but rather pleased to be asked for help again.

'What a happy coincidence, Polly; I've decided to write my

autobiography, and I could do with someone to put the material together for me – letters and documents, you know, there must be thousands of them all stacked away here somewhere. Just as long as he doesn't go quoting the Bible at me, of course. I'll try him out.'

'Oh, Felicity, I'm so glad about the book. I'll come and see you soon, and bring Jess – she's getting huge – and I still haven't thanked you properly for finding her.'

Upstairs they were asleep, family, friends – they were all sorted out now, they could manage. Polly felt she needed a holiday; she'd been with too many people for too long, community life had never suited her. She could go to the château, but Sandra was probably in charge of the village by now; she might sell it, if Muffy agreed. Suddenly the memory of the Norwegian pictures came back to her – the cold light, the empty spaces, the solitude. There was somewhere she would like to go. But alone? There was no reason why she, too, shouldn't have her own person.

Along the passage, the glass eyes of the rocking-horse glowed red in the reflected light. Polly gave him a pat, took down a coat and made her way across the fields to Toby's house.